THE BLONDE HURRICANE

THE BLONDE HURRICANE

by Jenő Rejtő

CORVINA

Published in Hungary 2003 by
Corvina Books Ltd.
Vörösmarty tér 1.
1051 Budapest

Translated from *A szőke ciklon*
by István Farkas
Translation revised by
Elisabeth West

Copyright © Heirs of Jenő Rejtő
English translation © István Farkas

Third edition

ISBN 963 13 5285 4

CONTENTS

PREFACE. *Contritely but briefly, the author confesses that his story has some antecedents.*

Acknowledgements are something which readers as well as authors like to get over quickly. That sort of thing is really very tedious. Very trite too, especially nowadays, when certain types of novel are simply manufactured from a formula just like new dishes devised from old recipes by a painstaking housewife. For instance: "Take two youthful loving hearts. Proceed to break them. Bring passions to the boil. Sprinkle with some sweet church blessing. Cook thoroughly or half-bake. Suitable for all occasions."

Perhaps I'd better stop beating about the bush and tell prospective readers straight away that, before they can settle down to enjoy the story that follows, there is this disagreeable question of acknowledgements to be dealt with. So let's get it over—the sooner the better. Here, then, are the ingredients from which our novel must be produced:

Take a bright young girl who tries to make a living by translating ballads—and when we say this it must be understood that she isn't living in clover: statistics relating to the social background of the financial oligarchy of the world demonstrate that the number of plutocrats who have made their pile by translating ballads is incredibly small. Next, take an aged convict. Proceed to cleanse his heart of all sin until the precious stone of genuine charity shines forth from its most hidden recesses. This precious stone is worth, at a conservative estimate, one million pounds sterling. This aged convict—Jim Hogan by name—and the said young girl's late father, Mr. Weston, were at school together. Mr. Weston used to make occasional visits to his convict friend and would from time to time send in food parcels for him: in a word, he did his best to alleviate Jim Hogan's unfortunate lot. After Mr. Weston's death, his family continued the charitable work and the aged prisoner thus continued to receive his food parcels while the occasional visits were now paid him by the late Mr. Weston's daughter, Evelyn.

We also need a light-pursed, moony young man who goes by the name of Eddie Rancing. He tenants the garret room next door to the Westons'. As for his occupation, he is working on an invention—a device to be fitted on motorcycles—which, when completed, should bring in millions. His work has by now reached an advanced stage in which all the details are on his designing desk, though there is still a certain vagueness as to the main purpose of the device. Young Rancing, thanks to an allowance from his guardian and uncle, Mr. Arthur Rancing, read law for the space of about two terms, but has lately taken to gambling and has fallen into the habit of getting through his allowance during the first four days of the months. His leisure-hours young Rancing devotes to being in love with Evelyn Weston—a sentiment which, at the beginning of our story, is still unrequited.

I also have to introduce to you Mr. Charles Gordon, an enterprising gentleman preparing to leave very shortly the penitentiary institution where he had been sent for a term of six years. Five years and three hundred and sixty-two days Mr. Gordon has taken in his stride, so to speak, but now, for some reason, this whole prison business is beginning to get on his nerves. We all have these moods at times. I know a rambler and mountain-climber, a fellow mostly to be seen with rucksack and alpenstock, sporting an edelweiss or gentian in his hat, one who looks upon the summit of Mont Blanc as a sort of second home. Last week, this man, no doubt in one of these uncontrollable fits of passion, gave the porter a sock on the jaw when he discovered that, for the second time in a month, the lift was out of order and he would have to shin it up to the fifth floor. Similarly, with only three days to go before his release, Charles Gordon complained of racking headaches and an abnormally rapid heart-action, whereupon a sympathetic prison doctor sent him to hospital.

CHAPTER ONE. *A millionaire lays down the glue-pot for good. He makes his will, disposing of his property, which is not far to seek: it must be somewhere on this earth. Even walls have ears—in the head of Eddy Rancing. His plan is to rob the girl, so that* he *can then make* her *rich. Exit Eddy Rancing. The Governor describes a prisoner 6ft. 3in. in height, with a disfiguring scar on his nose, who just possibly was not sleeping. Too bad!*

•1•

The millionaire, pail in hand, halted for a second.

The next instant he deeply regretted his momentary pause for a vigorous shove from behind reminded him that he must get a move on because the men in the workshop were waiting for him. The millionaire's arrival with the glue-pail was indeed being awaited by his fellow inmates. They were endeavouring to while away their time by making paper-bags and for this pastime were dependent on a steady supply of glue, which they obtained from our manhandled millionaire.

This affluent gentleman noted the fact that he had been given a push with an indifference ill-becoming a man of his social class. For the millionaire, fantastic as this may sound, was an inmate of the British prison of Dartmoor. This had been his abode for the last eight years, yet the fact that he was a millionaire was not known to anyone. Most people knew little about him beyond the fact that he was a rather stand-offish, tongue-tied old bird, somewhat on the heavy-handed side, who, at a venerable age, after a service record of full thirty years in the field of crime, had been sent into well-deserved retirement, with board and lodging for life, at Dartmoor.

Here he lived the unexciting, peaceful life of the retired criminal, dividing his day between cleaning his cell, taking a walk in the prison yard, and gluing paper-bags; and there were the occasional food parcels and visitors. Old Jimmy Hogan had only one visitor: Miss Evelyn Weston. After his former school-mate had departed this life, the daughter of the deceased continued to visit him once every two months. On these occasions, conversation between caller and host was not as a rule very spirited: the young lady would venture a few remarks to which he would respond with a mutter and a scowl.

Miss Weston was a student of literature and philosophy—a circumstance which bespeaks little practical common sense in a young lady. That may seem odd but it's a fact. It is just those who acquire their wisdom from the greatest philosophers who are most incapable of turning their ideas to good advantage. Evelyn Weston, for instance, was trying to earn a livelihood by translating old French ballads into English. If you consider that at the time of our story England was being rocked to the foundations by a dramatic slump in the demand for translations of old French ballads, you will not be surprised to learn that Mr. Weston's death hardly enabled them to make ends meet. Fortunately Mrs. Weston's brother contributed sums of varying amounts to meet their household expenses. This brother—Mr. Bradford, bespoke tailor for gentlemen—though not a wealthy man, was tolerably well provided with the necessary, owing to the fact that, besides plying his trade, he engaged in business speculations which were invariably successful.

I have thought it necessary to give you these facts so that you may the better appreciate the measure of Evelyn Weston's unselfishness in not letting old sinner Hogan down, for all her modest means.

·2·

When Jim Hogan had done fifteen years in jail, his case was brought before the Highest Court of all; and at this ultimate resort, nothing but acquittals are ever pronounced. Old Hogan waited in the prison hospital for release from human bondage; and as he was to stand before an Authority in whose judgment the most monstrous crime is dwarfed by the smallest good deed, he could be confident that in a matter of hours he would obtain his discharge from Dartmoor. At eight o'clock in the evening, an unusual thing happened. Old Hogan declared that he wanted to make his will. At first, the doctor put it down to the patient's high temperature. What could an old lifer possibly possess that he should need a will to dispose of it? His body would be committed to earth, his soul to hell, and his clothes consigned to the prison stores. However, as the prisoner persisted in his strange wish, and as even prison governors seldom refuse to grant a dying man's last request, the old gentleman's final disposition was put on record—in the presence of the chaplain and the governor, in compliance with his wish.

Next morning, old Jim Hogan was sitting on the ring of Saturn, dangling his feet cheerfully. He looked back at our dyspeptic planet from a distance of several thousand light-years, and rubbed his hands contentedly.

He had left to Miss Evelyn Weston the sum of approximately one million pounds.

·3·

I think it is unfair to judge people by their foibles. Nor do I consider curiosity a sin. It may have killed the cat or it mayn't (we know for certain that it has killed very few people, if any), but it isn't a sin. However, curiosity has a rather ugly twin sister or wild offshoot—eavesdropping. Eavesdroppers I despise. Every time I've caught myself eavesdropping I've had a guilty conscience which haunted me for minutes on end. There is something about this action which resembles assassination: It's as if you, with your organ of hearing, were stabbing other people's secrets in the back. One cannot therefore condone the sneaky behaviour of Eddie Rancing, even though the poor chap happened to be head over ears in love—a condition in which we all know that even the most adamant of male hearts is liable to be eroded. (Besides, mind you, young Eddie's heart, even at its stoutest, needed little eroding to be turned into the washiest mash ever prepared for greedy infant lips.)

And so we now find Eddie Rancing eavesdropping. Garret rooms are partitioned by walls so thin that for this operation he had only to press his ear to the wall-paper to be able to hear every word that passed between Evelyn Weston and her mother next door. Later on, he glued himself more and more adhesively on to the wall and would fain have pressed his other ear to it as well, had not a killjoy Nature rendered such a feat totally impossible. Luckily for him, he could hear everything distinctly enough even with one ear.

Evelyn was reading a letter to her mother. It was old Jim Hogan's last will and it had arrived by the afternoon post.

"...The undersigned, (Evelyn read), at the request of James Hogan, convict, readily certify herewith that in our opinion as well as that of the prison doctor, the aforenamed convict was *compos mentis* and, despite his illness, in full possession of his faculties when he dictated the testamentary disposition below, the authenticity whereof he has confirmed by his signature hereunto affixed.

"The Rev. G. H. Gladstone. M. Crickley. The Governor

"I hereby bequeath my property to the value of one million pounds to Miss Evelyn Weston, daughter of the late Samuel Weston, of King's Road, London. This property, worth one million pounds sterling, is a walnut-sized diamond which was presented to me as a gift. This may sound rather improbable and extraordinary, but then it was at a time of improbable and extraordinary happenings when it came into my possession. At the end of the war, in 1919, together with certain other British servicemen, I joined General Kolchak's counter-revolutionary army. When the campaign in Siberia had ended, I managed to make my way back to the European part of Russia after incredible hardships and suffering. Armed with the papers of a dead Austrian prisoner-of-war, I managed to get into a POW train and in this manner reached Moscow. Here, I ganged up with a number of people of my ilk and floated a company whose main line of business concerned the robbing of panic-stricken propertied types who were trying to flee the country. Our custom was to nose out a few such people and offer to smuggle them across the border into Poland for which purpose we had thoughtfully provided ourselves with an army lorry. Then, at some out-of-the-way place, we would simply swipe all their possessions and leave them in the road. In this way an old gentleman, short, white-haired and bearded, a soft-spoken old fellow and our very last passenger, was caught in our trap. He promised us a fabulous sum of money if we would smuggle him into Poland: he said he would give us a round sum of fifty thousand dollars! That day, we carried no other passengers but him: we put the old man into the lorry together with all his bags and boxes, and drove him a distance of some 200 *versts*, to a place where the highway ran through snow-bound woods. There we robbed him. That is to say, we would have robbed him, but we couldn't. Our passenger's luggage consisted of clothing, books and other worthless stuff. There was nothing to be gained by slashing the lining of his coat, or smashing up his chest: the man had no money on him at all. My three mates rounded on him: where was he going to get the fifty thousand dollars with which to pay us? 'I will pay you more than that,' said the passenger, 'if you will take me across the border. My property isn't in Russia any more.' One of my mates whipped out his knife and would have stabbed the old man there and then if I had not pushed him aside. I have no reason now to try and whitewash myself; I was a crook and a cad and, if there was any danger of my being caught doing a job, I would not have hesitated to use a knife. But one thing I insist on; namely, that never, at no time, did I ever become entirely incapable of humane feeling. I would not allow that old man to be massacred before my very eyes. There ensued an altercation which led to blows, and in the end my partners thrust me as well as the old man out of the lorry, and they all rumbled off. I shall not go into a deadline account of how we got to the Polish border making our way past small towns and lonely farmsteads. The only fact that has any relevance to my present story is that we finally reached the crucial stage of our journey where we found ourselves in what was called the 'neutral zone'—a strip of land several kilometres wide that separated the two countries during the peace talks. It was a severe winter; and here was I roaming about in the snow, ill-equipped, with one arm wounded, and saddled with a weary old man. 'You will see, sir,' he kept repeating, apparently under the illusion that he was boosting my moral, 'that once we're out of this alive, I will make you rich.' It was touch and go I didn't beat him up. I did give him ticking off. 'Ah, stop gassing,' I said, 'why, you haven't got anything besides those blessed trousers you're wearing!' I can still see his face as he looked at me. 'You're wrong.' he said. 'I have jewels that are worth millions—in a safe place in Paris. You see, my son got away safely in good time. It's the truth. Name your own price—and don't be modest.' I was getting hotter and hotter under the collar. 'You know what?' I shouted at him. 'Let's come to some arrangement here and now in this snow-storm. Let's say that you will one day bring to me in London the most precious piece from your family jewels. It'll be worth your while, I'm sure.' He quietly nodded. 'If you and I manage to survive, I'll bring the most valuable item of my family jewels to you in London. I shall be sorry to part with that particular jewel though; for it was the finest diamond in the Tsar's old crown.' You can well imagine what I answered to that. Funnels of snow were being sucked past us on every side; we were nearly knocked off our feet by the force of the gale; and distant howls of wolves made the whole scene unforgettably fearsome. We lost our way and could only wander on as if in a nightmare. We staggered on and were at the end of our strength when we found a cart-track in the snow. On the last stretch, I had to support the old man with my wounded arm, while I was hardly able to drag my own body along. Still, I should not have had it in me to leave him lying in that frozen, white desert. I gnashed my teeth, and fumed, but I lugged him along. At last, we were intercepted by Polish frontier police. My travelling companion was taken to the nearest hospital in a serious condition. Our ordeal had taken a good deal out of me too, and I had to drain a whole bottle of vodka to get right again. I packed myself among a load of refugees in a goods waggon heading for Danzig, where I went on board a British cruiser and so returned to England. And I never gave that old man another thought. Back in London, I soon got in touch with my old pals, and we got down to work without delay. After a few successful burglaries, we managed to get caught and sent to jail. And because I was an old lag I got two years, although they could not prove me guilty of more than one case of burglary. My solicitor warned me that when I was released I should think twice before getting myself involved in anything again because if I was brought to trial again, I would be sure to get the maximum sentence. But what can you do when you're on the wrong side of forty and have never tried your hand at anything except robbing and stealing? Four days after I had been released from prison, I broke into Selwyn's Department Store. If only I had waited one more day! If I had hesitated for another twenty-four hours I should now be ending my life as a wealthy gentleman enjoying my freedom instead of dying as I am, serving a life sentence down to the last minute. Just as I was looting the stuff, the night watchman arrived and caught me in the act. There was a bit of a struggle and in the end I stabbed him and fled. I thought I'd killed him. I decided that I'd have to pack up my traps and get out of England. I felt sure that when they discovered the murder in the morning it would be me that they'd suspect. It never occurred to me that the police would be on my trail that very night. Yet that was what happened. The night watchman was not dead: though seriously wounded, he dragged himself to the alarm bell. Within a few minutes, the police were there. Even the superficial description they obtained from the wounded man was enough for them to identify me. But I knew nothing of all this. I believed that I killed the watchman and that I had ample time to make a getaway before the store was opened, I had lodgings at 8, Lyndham Street, and the ground floor of the next house was a fancy-goods shop which specialised in ceramics and little figurines. The name of the firm is Longson & North. Please note the name carefully..."

Eddy, without removing his ear from the wall, whisked out a pencil and hurriedly scribbled the address on the wall-paper.

"It's an amazing story," said Evelyn.

"Go on," Mrs. Weston whispered excitedly. Evelyn continued reading the letter, and Eddy his eavesdropping.

"...I hurried home. The first surprise was waiting for me in front of the house, where I found a flashy, great limousine parked at the kerb although it was by now the middle of the night! I entered my room—and found myself face to face with the elderly gentleman I had helped to escape into Poland. He was sitting at the table—but how he had changed! His eyes were shining and his face, which I remembered as sad and sallow, now wore a friendly expression and there was about him an air of quiet authority. He was very neatly dressed; his hat and cane lay on the table before him.. He rose and came towards me, beaming.

"'We have a little account to settle if I remember aright,' he said. 'Let me introduce myself at last. I am Prince Radovsky. I should have shown up long ago, but I was seriously ill and bedridden for quite a long time. And afterwards, I found it extremely difficult to trace your place of residence.'

"I stammered something. He placed his hand on my shoulder, and with the cheery manner of someone about to make a good joke, continued: 'I've come to pay my fare; though what you did for me is something that can't be paid for in diamonds. As far as I can remember, you said you'd like to have the most precious of my family jewels?'

"He handed me a small black case containing a diamond. I had never seen such a large diamond of the first water and I don't think there are many other like it in the world. I was quite fascinated by it and stood there gaping, all thought of the murder and my escape driven from my mind.

"'I told you then that I was reluctant to part with this diamond because it came from the Tsar's old crown. But that, of course, must be no reason for me to break my promise. The members of my noble family will at any time readily attest that this diamond is Jim Hogan's rightful property which he acquired in an honest way.'

" 'Tha—thanks,' I stammered stupidly.

" 'Don't mention it,' he replied. 'This diamond is a meagre reward for your services. Good-bye.'

"He shook hands with me, and left. Out in the street, the engine of the car hummed. I gazed after it from the window—and none too soon a large car pulled up behind the prince's and began discharge policemen and detectives. It was a tragicomical situation. Here I was, with a priceless diamond in my hand—a robber and a murderer with the police hot on my trail. I had only one second in which to think. I knew that the diamond would still be mine even if I was arrested. But I also knew just how many people whom I had robbed would come forward to claim damages as soon as they learned that Jim Hogan owned a diamond worth a mint of money! I had to hide it! But where?... The cops might be already swarming up the stairs. I looked around; at that moment, the bell rang. I jumped through the bathroom window into the light well. There was an open window in the farther wall and I climbed in. I found myself in a large room littered with packing cases, shavings and wrapping paper. I heard a shot fired behind me and I ran on. In the adjoining room, the light of dawn filtered in through a window giving onto the street, and so I was able to get my bearings. I was in the workshop attached to the fancy-goods store. In a corner of the room, there was a bulky oven which had been bricked in: I was cornered. Through the shop window I could see the patrol car still standing in the street, with half a dozen detectives hanging around waiting to catch sight of me popping up somewhere. I noticed some half-finished statuettes on a desk... one of them a small Buddha surmounting an enamelled box. I touched it accidentally and found that the material was still soft. Swiftly I began to knead the diamond into the soft clay of the Buddha statuette, and then I smoothed over the surface to remove all traces of what I'd done. I was compelled to part with the diamond and to have enough faith in my own ingenuity to believe that one day if I was ever released from prison I should be able to trace the enamelled box with the ceramic statuette. In the meantime, the statuette might get broken and some other person get hold of the diamond; but at least there was a chance that I would lay hands on it myself. Big firms like this no doubt kept records of their sales, and I would be able to find some clue that would lead me to the statuette. I would have to check about fifty people, not an impossible task, I reckoned, even after the passage of ten years. A few minutes later, I was rushed in the police car to Scotland Yard. The night watchman did not die, but they gave me a life sentence all the same. For years, I clung to the hope that I might manage to escape or be granted a pardon; then I could go in search of the little Buddha sitting on the enamelled case. Now my last earthly chance has gone and I do not want to take the secret with me to the grave. I leave the diamond to Miss Evelyn Weston, and I trust that she will be able to find the Buddha containing it; if necessary, Prince Radovsky's family will testify that I acquired it in an absolutely honest way. The time has long since gone by when the victims of my early crimes could claim damages against the value of the diamond. Miss Weston should find the name of the person—or persons—to whom one or more cases of boxes decorated with figures of Buddha were sold from May 9th, 1922, onwards. The statuette represented Buddha in a most unusual posture: not the conventional sitting position with a straight back but with the trunk bent from the waist and the head bowed low. I know that the firm Longson & North is still in the business. That will make the first step easier for her. I am grateful to Miss Weston and her family for their charity and kindness to an undeserving man. God bless them, and may He have mercy on me.

James Hogan"

Eddy had heard enough. He clapped his hat on his head and dashed for the door. What luck! His uncle happened to be in London! He would touch him for a useful sum; the old bounder was sure to unbelt! Then he would seize the diamond from under Evelyn's very nose and present it to her as a gift! To a fellow of Eddy Rancing's wit and cheek, it would be mere child's play to beat the girl from scratch. And once he was rich, she would certainly not persist in her obstinate refusal to marry him! Two diamonds with one stone!

He buzzed off.

But it would have been better for him had he continued eavesdropping a little longer; for with the convict's last will, the governor of the prison had enclosed a private letter addressed to the executors, as follows:

"I feel it is my duty to inform you that while the present will was being recorded, a prisoner was lying in the adjoining ward (which we had supposed to be empty) who later claimed that he had been sleeping and heard nothing of James Hogan's confession. However, we have strong reason to suppose that the said prisoner, Charles Gordon (who at the moment is serving a sentence of six years for forging cheques) was *not* sleeping, but was eavesdropping and in thus possibly aware of the content of the said will.

"I hasten to inform you of this circumstance because the aforenamed prisoner's term expires tomorrow and, once released, he is likely to make a violent and unlawful attempt to gain possession of the estate of the deceased, the late James Hogan. Charles Gordon is 6ft. 3in. in height, totally bald, and inclined to obesity. He can be recognised by a disfiguring scar across his nose, the result of an injury sustained years ago.

"In apprising you of these facts..."

Mrs. Weston and her daughter looked at each other in bewilderment. They scarcely knew whether to be pleased or otherwise by this news of the legacy. The treasure had been immured in a piece of pottery made sixteen years ago! Who could say what had become of it by now? It might have been smashed to smithereens long ago. Or, if it was still in one piece, who knew in what lumber-room it might have been stowed away?

"Before we do anything," Evelyn declared firmly, "I think we'd better go and see Uncle Marius."

CHAPTER TWO. *Evelyn and her mother go to see Uncle Marius. Fortunately, Mr. North had always taken proper care of his internal organs and so the filing-clerk can now look forward to retirement and spending gay week-ends in the company of pretty women on the Continent. He devises a plan for marketing old sales ledgers, but shortly afterwards is attacked by an ex-convict. In Mr. Bradford's view Fate is like a boozy tailor. At this point, everybody leaves London; and Evelyn steps out of a pool of mud before going on board.*

·1·

Mr. Marius Bradford had just closed the door of the fitting-room behind his last customer when Miss Weston arrived with her mother. Mr. Bradford was fond of his sister but he was even more attached to his niece. Since the death of his brother-in-law, he had done his best to act like a father to her. In point of fact, he was now the head of the family. For this reason, Evelyn and her mother, whenever they called on Mr. Bradford, would attach very great importance to anything he said. So now it was with a grave and ceremonious air that he placed old Hogan's will before him and fished his spectacles from his breast-pocket. He read the document with concentrated attention.

"It seems to me," he said after much silent deliberation, "that this Jim Hogan must have been inveterately work-shy. I recently had in my employment an assistant who was a wonderful worker. He could face a topcoat, that fellow—something amazing. And yet I have been reluctantly compelled to fire him because the man is a boozer. That sort of thing is something I won't have. Why, this very morning, Lord Otterburn—he's one of my regular customers, you know—he said: 'Look, Mr. Bradford, as things are at present...'"

Evelyn interrupted him impatiently.

"Uncle," she said, "we've come here for your advice. What are we to do? That crook's going to be released tomorrow! We must do something immediately to forestall him..."

"Didn't I tell you that old Mr. North, of Longson & North, is an old customer of mine? I used to make poor Mr. Longson's clothes too. He died two years ago because of a neglected gallstone... All right, all right... I'll ring him up. He will be in at this hour, I except... Hallo! This is Mr. Bradford. Good afternoon, Mr. North. How do you like your new covert-coat?... I beg your pardon?... Oh no, I should say that's impossible. I only recommend a first-class cloth like that to old customers... No, not about that, Mr. North. Er—I wonder if you can tell me the name of the person to whom you sold that statuette with the big diamond seventeen years ago... Please, Mr. North! No, I haven't. Never in my life! I recently sacked my assistant for that very reason, sir... I'll hand the receiver to my sister's daughter; she's very anxious to have a word with you..."

Evelyn managed to seize the receiver.

"This is Evelyn Weston. So sorry for this intrusion, Mr. North. I am seeking information about a statuette sold by your firm some years ago... I beg your pardon? Oh. Could you give me the man's address please?"

She made a note on the margin of a fashion magazine lying beside her on the table, as she repeated the address:

"Austin Knickerbock... Number 4, Long Street... Thank you very much indeed, Mr. North. Good-bye."

She hung up.

"There," said Mr. Bradford. "You see, you needn't jump at the drop of a hat, my dear. I will now continue to direct this business..."

"Mr. North says," Evelyn interrupted, "that they have an old filing-clerk who writes circulars and calls on old customers soliciting orders. For this purpose he keeps the sales ledgers in his own home. There we can find all the old books belonging to the firm. The man's name is Austin Knickerbock and he lives at 4, Long Street. Let's go and look this fellow up straight away. We may even find him in now. That convict will soon be on the same track if he is really going to try to get hold of the diamond."

"A very sensible plan," Mr. Bradford agreed. "It's the tailor who hesitates who makes a bad fit not the one who boldly shears away at his cloth."

Mr. Bradford liked to illustrate his views with similes borrowed from the domain of sartorial art. He was just about to utter a maxim concerning the striking similarities to be observed between bad hats—figuratively speaking—and ready-to-wear morning coats, but Evelyn, assisted by Mrs. Weston, quickly extinguished the flow with his hat, which together they thrust onto his head prior to jerking him out into the street.

•2•

Number 4, Long Street was a dismal-looking three-storey tenement house. Mr. North's filing-clerk rented two evil-smelling holes at the end of a dark passage facing the courtyard. Like most elderly filing-clerks, Austin Knickerbock was a bachelor and a victim of melancholia. Wearing owlish spectacles to protect his eyes and alpaca cuffs to protect his jacket, he spent his days surrounded by old ledgers and files, writing to lapsed customers, whose names he copied out from the sales ledgers dating back to the vintage years, in the hope that they would order more fancy goods. He would send out circulars, mildly reproving in tone, pointing out the necessity for anyone claiming to be a cultured member of contemporary society to demonstrate this by furnishing his home with artistic statuettes, choice pottery and beautiful imitation Chinese vases. He pointed out that those who neglect to decorate their homes with such fancy goods, are liable to be avoided by their acquaintances and dropped by their friends.

A living proof of this argument was Knickerbock himself. His home was totally devoid of statuettes, his shelves empty of pottery items, and as to Chinese vases—imitation or otherwise—there was not one in sight. On the contrary, there were thick tufts of horsehair erupting from the ancient leather couch on which he slept; and he had his meals brought in from a cook-shop across the street. Only in one respect was the simile inappropriate. Knickerbock was not avoided by his friends. He had no friends at all.

In these circumstances, it is not surprising that Mr. Bradford and the two ladies, arriving as they did at such an unlikely hour of the night, should be greeted by a somewhat suspicious Knickerbock. His suspicions were multiplied when Mr. Bradford produced a ten-shilling note. Greed momentarily elongated the clerk's face and there appeared in his eyes the unmistakable glint of money-lust. Nevertheless, he mastered his urge to grab the stuff and decided to hear out any explanation that might be forthcoming.

"I am sorry," he said in a cool, business-like tone of voice after the proposition had been laid bare before him." These things are more valuable than you seem to think. You're not the first people to show an interest in this book," he added with instinctive cunning, and saw that his random shot had hit the target.

"You've sold it?" Evelyn gasped.

"No—not yet. I told the other fellow that I could not possibly let him have it for anything under fifty pounds, and he immediately rushed off to fetch the money."

"Here you are!" cried Mr. Bradford and he handed the clerk a cheque for fifty pounds.

Knickerbock hadn't the audacity to ask for more. He showed the visitors into the other room, where the prevailing odour was not unlike that of Roman catacombs. From a high shelf just below the ceiling, he fished out the sales ledger for 1922. It was a rather shabby volume; and as he lifted it off the shelf, the label came off and fell to the floor. Knickerbock, seeing no further point in keeping up the pretence of coolness, showed himself in a more helpful mood and reached obligingly for the glue-pot.

"Shall I paste the label back on for you?"

"No! no!" the visitors protested in unison: and, seizing the ledger, left the premises in great haste, closing the door behind them.

Left to himself again, Knickerbock first switched off the light for reason of economy; he then sat down on his leather couch, which creaked plaintively, and lit a thin dark-brown cigar. Absently, he puffed out the smoke. Well! Thank Heaven, at last a poor filing-clerk had been noticed by someone in this rotten world in which it had always seemed that the old grease was only applied to civil servants' palms. Graft was a nice thing, after all. He puffed at his cigar, deeply moved, and fell into a reverie as blissful as that of any young mother. He was startled out of his day-dream by the sudden ringing of the door-bell.

"Who on earth can it be this time?" he wondered.

First he switched on the light. Then he moved to answer the bell and as he did so he was invaded by a curious feeling, a kind of premonition. He opened the door, and immediately was thrust aside by a young man who rushed into the house in a state of great agitation, shouting excitedly.

"I've been speaking with your boss on the phone," began the young man hurriedly. "Mr. North said that other people had been making inquiries, too... Tell me, has anyone else been here yet?"

Knickerbock felt a rush of soothing warmth about his heart. Well, well. You never could tell. Misfortunes, as anyone would tell you, never come singly. But perhaps the same rule applied to fortunes too. If this young fellow had come here to bride him too, he certainly would feel no surprise.

"What can I do for you?" he asked cautiously.

"My name is Edward Rancing. I've come to buy your sales ledger for the year 1922," he said, and he let Knickerbock catch a glimpse of the hundred-pound note he was clutching in one hand.

"If you please, sir," Knickerbock bleated miserably, almost in tears; "are you sure you must have the volume for 1922, of all years? I have all the volumes, from 1878 down to the present day, including two volumes for the year when war broke out 1914..."

"For heaven's sake, man, stop drivelling: Go and get the volume for 1922 immediately and I'll give you one hundred pounds for it!"

Knickerbock's suspicions were now multiplied a thousandfold. Those rascals had cheated him! They had taken an unfair advantage of him! They had counted on his sense of fair play! That ledger must contain some information of very great value. But he would not leave it at that! Tomorrow morning he would go to the police! For the time being, he would take a few soundings to see just how much that book was worth.

"I am sorry, sir," he said, "A few minutes ago, some persons came here and offered to pay two hundred pounds for the book. They've just gone to fetch the money. But I'll charge you less for any of the other books. I could let you have all the rest at a bargain price."

"Look," panted Rancing. "I'll pay you two hundred and fifty, cash down here and now."

The clerk stood transfixed. He felt a lump in his throat and for a few seconds he really thought he would choke. He would certainly have to inform the police!

"Man alive!" yelled the young man suddenly, misinterpreting Knickerbock's silence as hesitation. "Look! I'll give you three hundred pounds! Bring me the book quickly!" For Eddy was afraid he might run into the Westons, and in the same breath he increased his bid: "Three hundred and fifty!"

Knickerbock staggered into the other room, dumb with amazement. He felt like a Corsican baron returning from a tour of inspection of his tenants and serfs to find his ancestral castle burnt to the ground by his foes, and his family kidnapped or murdered (or having suffered whatever fate was decreed by the rules then in force between noble enemies). The bloodsuckers! They had got that prize for fifty pounds! For a song! He had not known what he was giving away.

Did he know now?

He did.

He now knew that he'd thrown three hundred pounds down the drain. He had thrown away the biggest chance of his life!... He stared wildly round—and saw the label on the floor:

LEDGER-BOOK FOR 1922

Here was his salvation: He snatched up the label, seized the first ledger he could lay his hands on, which happened to be the volume for 1926, and in a matter of seconds, with the aid of the glue-brush, he had firmly pasted the fallen label over the original label.

It was all done in a trice, more swiftly than Knickerbock would ever have thought possible. The stained, old label with the inscription in black ink looked absolutely authentic. This particular ledger might not contain the one item which made the ledger for 1922 so covetable, but if the young man in the other room did not discover this slight adjustment until the following day, he would simply deny having received any money from him. He waited for the glue to dry, then returned to the other room with the book in his hand, saying ruefully:

"This is the book, sir. As a matter of fact, I gave my word to the person who was here before you—and a gentleman's honour..."

"Three hundred and fifty quids! Think of that!"

"My honour cannot be bought with three hundred and fifty pounds!"

"How much?" asked Eddy briefly.

"Four hundred. That's not much for a gentleman's honour." The next moment he had the four hundred pounds in his hand. But when the young man had left, Knickerbock no longer felt happy. He saw clearly that they were all taking advantage of his ignorance. That book must be worth a fortune. He would sue them, he would!

Gradually he became calmer, but he did not go to bed immediately. It was possible that other buyers might drop in yet. And now that he came to think of it, it should not be too difficult to alter the 7 on the label for 1927 and so manufacture yet another volume for 1922. In any case it might be as well to soak the labels off a few more ledgers, and change the figures. It would do no harm to be prepared.

Some time later, he lit another short black cigar with fingers that trembled a little. Graft was a nice thing after all. He would use half the money to gamble in stocks and shares, and he would lend the other half at an exorbitant rate of interest. Against good security, of course. He would not let anyone get the better of him. He would chuck up this dreary job. After all, he wasn't sixty yet: life had scarcely begun for him. Now he would be able to take week-ends on the Continent and get to know a few pretty young women. Knickerbock sat up until six in the morning. He could scarcely expect more visitors now, so he lay down on the couch for a little and dozed off immediately.

It was precisely five minutes later when he was rudely awakened by the shrill sound of the door-bell. He had been dreaming that, as general manager of a vast fancy-goods concern, he was giving the sack to a number of filing-clerks for not pulling their weight. Roused from this sweet dream, Knickerbock hurried to answer the bell. His early visitor proved to be a tall individual, over 6ft. in height, and slightly running to fat; he was somewhat bald and there was a disfiguring scar on his nose. He seemed to be in a very good humour, as well he might be, for he had come straight from Dartmoor.

"Hullo, old fellow!" was his cheery greeting. "What made you choose to live in this lonely out-of-the-way spot, eh? Why anyone could come and do you in here and no one the wiser."

"What can I do for you?" Knickerbock responded, his voice trembling slightly, for although he had been living in this 'lonely' spot for the last ten years, the possibility of being 'done in' had never occurred to him.

"Now look here. Let's talk business. I want your sales ledger for 1922 and I don't mind parting with some dough to get it."

"The question is," said Knickerbock, the astute businessman once more, "*how much* don't you mind parting with?" In his mind's eye, Knickerbock was already in the back room changing a certain number 7 into a 2. "I have just turned down an offer of one thousand pounds."

"Then you've made the biggest mistake of your life. Three bob's the most you can hope for from me. No! On second thoughts the cash offer is cancelled. You ain't going to get a brass farthing out of me. Either you give up the ledger or I'll give you something you won't forget in a hurry. Take your choice: Hand over the book or I'll hand you something harder." A powerful hand fell on Knickerbock's neck in a seemingly casual way. "I'm just out of Dartmoor. I've been in jug for six years. So I warn you, old fellow, I've even been so careless as to kill people in my time. Now you nip along and get that book for me. The ledger, my man and put some snap into it!"

Knickerbock's knees began to give beneath him; he had told a lie that might cost him his life.

"I was not speaking the truth," he whimpered. "I haven't got that ledger any more... I... I've sold it twice, to two different people."

"Come clean," thundered the towering visitor. "I want the whole story and don't try any monkey tricks with me. If you shout, you'll die. I have all my pals waiting for me outside."

With trembling fingers the clerk poured himself a glass of water, raised it to his lips and drank. Somewhat restored, he proceeded to tell the ex-prisoner what had happened, sticking to the truth this time because he knew that his life was at stake. Gordon could tell that this time the clerk was telling no lies. When the old man confessed how he had tampered with the date label on the second ledger, the ex-convict was scarcely able to suppress his mirth. When Knickerbock had finished his storey, a savage expression came over Gordon's face and he bawled:

"You lied to me, you worm! You'll die for it!" Knickerbock dropped to his knees in terror, and wrung his hands imploringly:

"I beseech you, sir... I have a family to support... I support my aunt who lives at Birkham in Sussex..." This was a desperate plea considering that he had not seen his aunt since the unhappy occasion eight years previously when they had quarrelled over a couple of silver candlesticks which both of them had felt the urge to remove from the home of a deceased relative. Realising the weakness of his argument, Knickerbock had the idea of strengthening it by actually producing the money.

"Look here," he said. "How do you suppose a poor filing-clerk like me comes to have four hundred and fifty pounds cash unless all that I've been telling you is true?"

With one sweeping gesture of his right arm the ex-prisoner scooped up the notes from the clerk's outstretched hand; for a moment it looked as if he was going to fling them all in the man's face, but the sweeping movement was broken abruptly as he stuffed the money in his pocket. Then he gave a perfect demonstration of a textbook left hook, beautifully aimed at the clerk's chin.

It was broad daylight Knickerbock recovered consciousness. Ruefully, he fingered his jaw, then—far more ruefully—his pocket. He had had four hundred and fifty pounds—in transit. That fabulous sum had rested in his pocket—for one night. Alas, it had been just another case of ships that pass in the night. Some minutes later he was astounded to discover the extent of the ex-convict's thoroughness for the man had also whisked away the two pounds which constituted Knickerbock's hard-won, legal earnings! His own money! A fragment of his wretched salary. It was to have kept him going till the first of the month! The accursed crook had left him penniless!

To lose the fabulous sum of four hundred and fifty pounds may be depressing, painful and grievous enough. But the loss of two hard-earned pounds is a terrible blow. It is a tragedy. That day Knickerbock opened his door to no one. He wrote to his landlord that he would be leaving his rooms; and he decided that he would continue to refrain from spending his week-ends on the Continent.

It was a wicked world he lived in; there were no moral standards in it. Graft was not nice, after all. Just let anyone come and try to bribe him again!

But Knickerbock waited for the occasion in vain. No prospective grafters ever came his way again.

•3•

How, you may wonder, had Eddy Rancing come by the fabulous sum of money which had stunned old Knickerbock? He had been getting round his uncle. Mr. Arthur Rancing lived in the country and, as a country gentleman, his attitude towards his impecunious metropolitan relatives was one of suspicion and distrust. His gravest suspicions were directed towards his nephew Edward. Now, having listened to young Edward's fantastic account of how he had overheard the convict's last will, he paced up and down for a long time, immersed in thought. After some time, he put a call through to Dartmoor Prison. By claiming to be a relative of James Hogan, he managed to acquire confirmation of the fact that the old convict was dead, and that, before dying, the late J. Hogan had made a will which the prison authorities had now forwarded to the executors. This piece of information settled it. The thought of a precious stone worth one million pounds sterling was stimulating enough to move the wealthy but close-fisted uncle to action. Miserly folk, once their suspicions have been overcome, often turn out to be the most reckless of gamblers.

"Look, uncle," Eddy explained. "This is just what the doctor ordered for me. This business calls for genius. Once I pick up the scent, I will be on to that diamond for you like a retriever after a quail. However, the operation will cost money. It may be some months before I succeed, I may have to bribe people. I may have to meet people and travel around. Altogether, it will take not a penny less than two thousand pounds. If you fork up the needful, I'll go halves with you."

"And suppose you try to cheat me?"

"Uncle! You know me."

"That's why I'm asking."

"Look. I'll give you an I.O.U. for five hundred thousand pounds. Once I've got hold of the diamond I'll want to enjoy my fortune. I shall go into business; I'll buy a house or an estate, and in any case you'll be able to pin me down with the I.O.U. When I've found the diamond I won't bury it in the earth; as soon as I've sold it and start using the money, you'll be able to claim your share. But you won't have to do that. I'm just as honest as you are. Besides, you know, dog doesn't eat dog."

Thus it happened that Fate brought Eddy Rancing the great chance of his life and, with two thousand pounds in his pocket, he went to see the filing-clerk and cheerfully carried off the ledger never suspecting that it was for the year 1926, and that the volume he wanted was in Evelyn's hands. As chance would have it, Longson & North had also sold one 'Dreaming Buddha' (as the precious statuette mounted on a box was called) in the year 1926. These statuettes had been made for the firm by a ceramic artist named Thompson, and fortunately he made only a limited number of each particular model. Two or, at the most, three 'Dreaming Buddhas' were sold each year, and when one had been sold, a new one would be ordered from Thompson. Unfortunately for Eddy, one 'Dreaming Buddha' mounted on a box had been sold, according to an entry in the bogus ledger, in May that year. The statuette, along with another item—a group called 'Harvesters'—was despatched on May 27th to Herr Adalbert Wollishoff, a technical adviser, Mügli am See, Switzerland.

Eddy Rancing therefore attempted to steal a march on his rivals for the treasure by flying to Zürich, whence he proceeded by the shortest possible route to that picturesque resort, Mügli am See.

•4•

Meanwhile Evelyn learned from the genuine ledger for 1922 that the little enamelled box with the ceramic ornament called 'Dreaming Buddha' had been supplied, as per order, to Lieutenant-Commander Terence Brandon, of 4, Westminster Road. The night was already well advanced, but Evelyn was anxious to make the most of their advantage in having been able to start several hours before the convict was to be released, even supposing that he was also in possession of the secret.

It was midnight when the cab in which Evelyn and her mother had travelled from the clerk's lodgings turned into Westminster Road. (Mr. Bradford had meantime gone home.) Evelyn rang the bell, and when presently the door opened they could just make out in the dim light of the hall first a pair of shuffling slippers, above them an expanse of snowy white robes visible as far as the knees of its owner and above them a dignified and braided mantle; the wearer of these garments had completed his attire with an elaborate cap so that he presented an appearance more in keeping with a land-lubber's idea of an admiral in dishabille than a janitor roused from bed.

"Yes?" queried the apparition.

"We wish to see Lieutenant-Commander Brandon," Evelyn replied. "Is he at home please?"

The man gaped at her in a dumbfounded sort of way as if she had been inquiring after Commander Christopher Columbus.

"You must be making some mistake!" he said when he had managed to return his jaw to a more normal position.

"Oh," said Evelyn, dismayed. "Surely he hasn't moved away from here?"

"That's just what he has done, I'm afraid. Yes. Good and proper, too. You don't seem to have read your newspaper very well, ma'am. It's less than a year since Commander Brandon was making front-page headlines every day."

She slipped a shilling into the dignified door-keeper's hand. "It seems that the affair has escaped my attention. I suppose you couldn't give me the board outlines of what happened to him?"

"Well, as a matter of fact, nobody knows the whole truth of the matter. They do say that he made off with some very important military documents. Yet he seemed such a decent, respectable tenant. Respected by all—held in general esteem, you know. Why, he misled even me! Me, being a door-keeper, it's part of my job to be a keen judge of character. For instance, I'm supposed to be able to tell whether a stranger walking into this building is visiting the actress on the third floor or a cat-burglar in his best clothes doing a bit of reconnoitring before getting down to his real work. Well, as I was saying, being a door-keeper in a big mansion means that I'm pretty well up in the art of placing people just by looking at them—but even I made a mistake over the commander."

It was a good job, thought Evelyn, that Uncle Marius was no longer with them, or the light of dawn might find still exchanging worldly commonplaces with this august commissionaire.

"Well, if I understand you correctly, Commander Brandon has been involved in a criminal case?"

"Up to the eyebrows. And, as I say, even I, a commissionaire..."

"Yes, yes, I know. Even you got quite a wrong impression on his character."

"Very happily put, ma'am. Most felicitously expressed. Why, even commissionaires are liable to make an occasional error of judgement. To err, ma'am—as my uncle Joseph never tired of pointing out—is a human failing; and, after all, we commissionaires are no less—and no more—human than any other people. My Uncle Joseph was a commissionaire too."

Evelyn sighed.

"It seems to be a sort of family calling."

"I wouldn't say that. Take my grandfather. He was Head Stableman to Lord Derby. Not to mention my kinswomen, whom their sex automatically prevented from entering the profession. True, some feminist voices have lately been heard raising the demand that, like other vocations, door-keeping be opened to women. But," and he looked intently at Evelyn, raising a warning finger, "if you ask me, this is a dream of the very, very distant future. This occupation, my dear lady, is one for men. It calls for keen eyes and a quick wit, for resource and an ability to act promptly."

"Yes, yes. To be sure... Now, I wonder, could you tell us something about Commander Brandon?"

"Well, on the face of it, he was as decent a person as ever lived in this house. A thoroughly decent fellow. However, one day, it seems, he got hold of some military documents, disappeared, and nothing has been seen of him since."

"He made off without warning, I suppose, leaving his things behind?"

"The commander's departure was indeed precipitous, ma'am. His flat stayed just as he left it for a long while before his mother had all his furniture and belongings removed."

"Could you tell us where we can find Mrs. Brandon, please? It's important for us to speak to her at once."

"That is virtually impossible since we have not yet reached the age of travel by rocket. At this moment, Mrs. Brandon happens to be in Paris."

"Oh," Evelyn heaved a sigh. "Has she gone to live in Paris then?"

"That's right," said the commissionaire. "Since the invention of the aeroplane, it has become possible to reach Paris within a comparatively short time. I well remember the years when such a trip used to be quite a serious undertaking."

"Could you give me Mrs. Brandon's address in Paris?"

The commissionaire shuffled back into his office. When he returned he was wearing wire-rimmed pince-nez, and was browsing in a note-book with chequered covers.

"Ah. Here it is! This is the address his furniture was sent to... Have you got a pencil? The best policy is to write such things down. One keeps forgetting addresses. Well, then... Mrs. Emily Brandon... Got it down?... Number 7, Rue Mazarin... Paris... France..."

"Thank you very much. Well, I must be going now. I'm in an awful hurry."

"Then I'll just hang about here a bit longer and I think I might have a gasper."

"I hope you enjoy yourself. Good-bye."

"Good-bye, ma'am. And—Bon voyage!"

•5•

Evelyn and her mother did not get a wink of sleep all night. A trip to Paris was no light matter for the Westons: travelling expenses, hotels, restaurants... "Oh, dear, we simply can't afford it," Mrs. Weston lamented. There had been a time when they would have thought nothing of "hopping over" to Paris: in those days the cost of such a trip would have seemed negligible.

In those days! Why, before the late Mr. Weston had begun to speculate in land with such unfortunate results, they had even had a car.

"Well," said Mrs. Weston, sighing, "if anyone can help us now, it will be Marius, as usual."

"You know, I have an idea that Uncle Marius won't let us down."

Nor was she mistaken. Next morning, Evelyn was standing in the pleasant fitting-room where the smell of freshly ironed clothes showed that the morning's work was already well advanced. Mr. Bradford was standing in front of a basted jacket on a dummy, scrutinising the work with an expert eye.

"You shall cross the Channel, my dear," he said as, head on one side and a few pins projecting from his lips, he took out a flat, round piece of chalk from his waistcoat pocket, and proceeded to mark the position of the buttons. "We will raise the money. We must get to the bottom of this business, whether we get any benefit from it or not. Destiny is like a drunken tailor, my dear: When he starts cutting a piece of cloth, there's no knowing whether it'll turn out as a topcoat or a pair of trousers. Two hundred pounds is all I have to spare at the moment, and that's what I'll give you to cover your expenses. It is my belief that there's been the divine hand at work over this business of the will—though I don't usually have much faith in that sort of thing. But I should never be able to sleep in peace if you did not have a go at finding that diamond. And sound sleep is essential for tailors—it's an absolute necessity for anyone engaged in hard mental work."

Evelyn, however, was no longer listening to her uncle.

She had chanced to look down through the window and her glance fell on a man on the sidewalk across the street: he was tall, bald-headed, and there was a disfiguring scar on his nose.

·6·

An unpleasant surprise awaited Lord Bannister, the well-known medical scientist, when he heaved himself out his elegantly low-slung Alfa-Romeo at Dover. A flock of journalists and cameramen had alighted on the quay where the boat for Calais lay berthed, and was lying in wait for him. His lordship, like most scientists, was a modest, retiring sort of person who hated publicity. Lord Bannister, though not yet forty, had an impressive record of scientific achievement behind him, and it was rumoured that he was going to be awarded a Nobel Prize for his outstanding discoveries about the treatment of sleeping-sickness. Recently, he had received from the royal hand one of the highest decorations in the land, and so much publicity had been given to his research work that he had now received the final accolade—popular interest in a scientific theory which no one really understood. Lord Bannister's sleeping-sickness theory (about "predestinate races") had made its triumphant entry, under the flying colours of intellectual snobbery, into clubs and tea parties, and every ambitious bank clerk managed to bring it into the conversation along with Psychoanalysis and Relativity. A few more yards and the race would be won; Lord Bannister's name would make headlines in the science-and-culture columns of the Sunday papers.

His lordship was leaving for Paris, where he had been invited to lecture at the Sorbonne University. From Paris, he would be going on to Morocco, where he had established a research unit for the study of tropical diseases. There, too, he had a large and beautiful villa in which he usually spent the greater part of the year. It was his present intention to stay in Morocco for the next six months for he was longing for a period of subtropical peace and solitude.

Lord Bannister was both serious and modest, a retiring, timid sort man.

But tragedy was not unknown to this modest intellectual. He was reputed to be unhappy in his private life. His brothers had died young, and his present trip marked the happy ending of an unhappy marriage: he had for some time been embroiled in a divorce suit and that very morning his marriage had been dissolved. Lord Bannister was glad that he had so far succeeded in keeping the painful affair secret. He lived in constant dread lest one or other of the newspapermen dogging his footsteps should one day find out that he was after all divorcing his wife.

One can understand, therefore, that when Lord Bannister stepped out of his car and after a few unsuspecting steps, found himself facing a barrage of flashlights, he actually leaped into the air like a jumping-bean. Thoroughly off guard, he reeled, stepped back and so tripped up a young lady immediately behind him who was also heading for the gangway. Down she went—suitcase, hat box and all—in the very middle of a pool of muddy water. The journalists, alarmed to see the disastrous result of their zeal, took to their heels. Lord Bannister was at a loss as to how he should behave in the circumstances. All his work in the field of medicine had not prepared him for such a contingency. The young lady, her elegant clothes quite ruined, now struggled to her feet, and fixed on the embarrassed scientist the accusing eyes of a martyr.

"I am awfully sorry," Lord Bannister stammered. "I...I would like to compensate you for all this damage... It was all my fault... my name is Bannister—er, er, Lord Bannister."

"The scientist!" she cried enthusiastically, forgetting that at that moment she presented the unfortunate appearance of a female chimney-sweep. "I am so very glad to meet you, Lord Bannister."

"The honour is mine," mumbled the noble scientist and, exercising some self-control, took the muddy hand which the enthusiastic young lady was holding out to him. "I'm very glad to... I mean, I'm frightfully sorry..."

In an awkward and embarrassed fashion, he began to extricate himself from his predicament. It had been his original intention to linger on the quayside to watch his car being loaded onto the ship, but now he had lost interest. He was really very angry with this clumsy girl. It was quite possible that the incident would be reported in the press. Good Lord! Was there anything left on earth that would *not* be reported in the press, he wondered. It was lucky they hadn't got wind of his divorce yet. His remaining hope now was that he would not meet any friends and acquaintances on board. This did not seem too extravagant a hope, considering that Lord Bannister was a man who gave out friendship in exceedingly small doses; with any luck he ought to be able to enjoy a quiet crossing, unmolested by bores asking fatuous question and wondering if he had read any good books lately.

Lord Bannister had no such luck. Indeed, it seemed that Fate was going out of her way to spite him; for he had only just emerged from the gangway and taken a few wary steps on deck when he ran into a massive fellow with a heavy jowl and thick, horn-rimmed spectacles who instantly greeted him in stentorian tones. (It would in fact have been more truthful to say that it was the loud-voiced gentleman who ran into Lord Bannister—literally ran into him for he had been walking at a good speed and the impact with which he came into contact with the unlucky peer was inconsiderable.) It was some moments before Lord Bannister was sufficiently recovered to be able to identify this sonorous mass of flesh as P. J. Holler, newspaper proprietor and Busybody of the First Order; his heart sank for the *Mindlands Mercury* and *Morning Clarion* were among the staunchest supporters of his scientific theories. Canadian by birth, Peter Jeremy Holler was only a junior reporter when he arrived in England where his shrewd business sense, ambition and energy soon earned him in Fleet Street the nickname "Pushing Jerry." It was not long before he was buying up newspapers and magazines, especially in the provinces. Since all his energies were ruthlessly directed towards the acquisition of newspapers, he now controlled nearly a hundred, and still the Moloch of his imprint demanded the sacrifice, one by one, of those papers still struggling to retain their independence.

There are business magnates whose ruthless and assertive methods are in strange contrast to their silent, unobtrusive manner when one meets them personally. It was not so with P. J. Holler. He used both fists when he went into the fight, and when he wanted to be friendly he demonstrated the fact with transatlantic heartiness and exuberant back-slapping. The amount of noise he made was almost offensive. In fact there are few people who can so adequately justify their names as "Pushing Jerry" Holler. From P. J. Holler's vocabulary, such words as *reticence, taciturnity* and their synonyms, appeared to be missing. Indeed, his qualities could best be described by their opposites—attributes which were scarcely destined to meet with Lord Bannister's approval. His lordship's idea of what constituted polite intercourse scarcely tallied with that of P. J. Holler; and so, as he now unexpectedly found himself face to face with the man, Lord Bannister winced and dejectedly closed his mental eyes. Here was the end of his hope to travel unrecognised. The man was a pest—and unfortunately not a mere everyday pest at all. There was nothing commonplace, drab or obscure about P. J. Holler; he attracted attention to himself wherever he went and it was inevitable that the hapless creature who happened to be in his company would receive a full share of that attention. Even now, as his resounding greeting boomed over the deck, Lord Bannister was only too painfully conscious that every member of the ship's company pricked up his ears and stared. It seemed to his lordship that he was the single tongue-tied actor on a stage watched by everyone on board.

And now Lord Bannister was horrified to learn that P. J. Holler usually spent his holidays in Africa and was now on his way to Morocco. He resigned himself to a minimum of ten minutes of idle talk with the press lord.

It certainly was true, thought Lord Bannister, that misfortunes never come singly, for he was just getting safely through his ten minutes of small talk when into sight hove another familiar-looking face: it belonged to the Mayor of Paris, who was returning from a visit to London by the same boat. *Monsieur le maire* knew Lord Bannister, as he had attended the ceremony at the Sorbonne when an honorary degree had been conferred upon the noble lord. The ten minutes thus had to be prolonged to a half-hour ordeal, made all the more trying by a cocktail and the mayor's chatty wife. Lord Bannister detested all garrulous wives and towards this one he had a particular aversion.

The mayor told his lordship the happy news that in all probability he would be elected as a member of that same league for the protection of public morals of which Lord Bannister was one of the sponsors. His lordship declared that it would be great pleasure to have *monsieur le maire* as a fellow member. Meantime Holler promised to break his journey in Paris so that he could attend his lordship's lecture. He would continue his journey to Morocco by air—it would be no trouble at all.

Now they found themselves besieged by autograph-hunters. These impudent fellows stood around grinning and gazing as if he were an animal in the zoo, or a *deb* at a coming-out ball. He stretched his face into an amiable grimace.

"Have you ever seen the sun rise over the Channel, Lord Bannister?"

That was the sort of idiotic question he was called upon to answer. It had been asked by Holler, of course, and he would certainly have to rustle up an answer.

"Er... the sun?... Over the Channel..." the scientist mused, casting about for some sort of reply. "I don't think I did... I mean, I should think... er... perhaps at some time..."

"Monsieur 'Oller and myself," the mayor butted in, "have agreed to stay up for the remaining three and a half hours to see the sun come up over the Channel."

"We are great lovers of nature," explained the chatty spouse.

"Oh really," commented his lordship.

"Lady Bannister is not coming down to dine?" asked Holler, for the gong had been rung, and the passengers were beginning to descend to the dining-saloon. The great scientist actually blushed. What more could he be called upon to endure?

"Lady Bannister?..." A look of intense suffering appeared briefly on his usually imperturbable countenance. "No, I don't think she will be able to take supper," he said sadly.

"It's just as well for her to stay in her state-room at the beginning of the crossing," the mayor remarked, soothingly.

Panic thoughts flitted through Lord Bannister's head, for he had never learned to tell a lie. Why hadn't he said coldly that his wife was still in London?

At dinner, it seemed that there was not a person on board who did not attempt to speak at least a couple of words to the celebrated scientist. At least he escaped to the boat deck and was just taking a deep breath of the free ocean air when the mayor clutched him by the elbow and begged his urgent presence in his state-room. A lamp flushed and Lord Bannister knew that his life was still being recorded for an avid public. Disgusted and weary as he was he scarcely noticed that the mayor was no longer with him when the mayor's wife, still chatting, began to unbutton her blouse, asking him to give a scientific assessment of the effect of the sun on her delicate skin.

It was midnight when he staggered back to the haven of his state-room.

At last, at last, he was alone.

He made tea (he never drank tea made by others), lowered himself wearily into a chair, lit a cigar and attempted to soothe his jarred nerves by reading. In his state of extreme exhaustion, it was a matter of seconds before he dozed off.

As he did so, the door of his state-room was flung open and there stood before him, wearing heliotrope pyjamas, the young lady last seen emerging from a pool of muddy water on the quayside at Dover. This young lady now fell upon Lord Bannister, shook him by the shoulder and addressed him in trembling tones, thus:

"My name is Evelyn Weston. Please allow me to spend the night here in your state-room..."

CHAPTER THREE. *The state-room lies in ruins. Lord Bannister is at a loss and Evelyn goes to sleep. Dawn shows them in an unfavourable light. The ex-prisoner, in spite of his excellent references, is compelled to go and look elsewhere for a job. Beefy commits an act of justifiable self-defence against a taxi driver, thus giving proof of his respectability. Gordon calls on Buddha at his home. Evelyn cancels Mr. Wilmington's supper, then lays the table.*

·1·

When Evelyn had at last removed the traces of her muddy adventure, she hurried into the saloon. She was ashamed that in the presence of the great scientist she had been so flustered, and had cast down her eyes like a silly schoolgirl. When she had finished her dinner, she went straight back to her cabin. She prepared to go to bed, but instead sat down by the porthole and read.

She had never before spent a night at sea. The Channel, as usual, was a bit rough, and she began to feel giddy. She therefore put down her book and went out to take a walk in the fresh air. It was a dark and foggy night and there was not another soul on deck.

She walked towards the stern and, feeling a little better, turned back. The ship seemed to be abandoned, as if she were the only passenger. Nor did she see a single deckhand. In the eerie silence she listened to her own footsteps. She began to hurry. She could hear the echo of her footsteps. Then her heart leapt into her mouth as she realised that the echo was ahead of her. She stopped dead in her track and saw at the end of the empty corridor a man waiting outside her cabin. It was the ex-convict!

Her hand flew to her heart, and she stifled the scream that rose to her lips. She began to reassure herself that she could not be attacked here, on a cross-channel boat. But all her reasoning was in vain. She was exhausted by the exciting events and now, alone, she gave way to panic.

Ahead, the bald-headed man continued to stand, feet wide apart, outside the door of her cabin, and for a fleeting second she made out the disfiguring scar on his nose.

With a sudden resolve, she moved forward, but faltered immediately as she saw with what determination her enemy remained at his post.

Under the door of the nearest state-room she could see a faint bar of light. Shuddering with fear, scarcely knowing what she was doing, breathless and blind with panic she flung open the door, fell upon the slumbering figure within, and said in trembling tones:

"My name is Evelyn Weston. Please allow me to spend the night here in your state-room... I am being followed!"

•2•

When Lord Bannister realised the identity of the young lady by whom he had been so rudely awakened, he could scarcely have been more perturbed had been confronted by the stuffed rhinoceros that dwelt in his London home and found himself invited by that animal to a friendly game of poker. In fact it would have been a welcome alternative to his present predicament for the eminent scientist was more likely to have known what to say to a card-playing rhino than to the lady in the heliotrope pyjamas who called herself Evelyn Weston, and was trying to run away from some great danger in her bedroom slippers.

However, there was one thing he knew he must do in the presence of a lady and that was to extricate himself from his chair forthwith; such an enterprise was not without its hazards and at his first cautious movement, his most persistent enemy, his tea-cup, crashed to the floor. At the same moment he found that the table-cloth was rising with him, suspended by a thread from his waistcoat so that the sugar basin and the spirit stove tumbled to one side while his book was flung to the other side taking with it a large bottle from which the friendly rum began to trickle across the floor of the cabin, lapping up the sugar as it went and soaking the carpet in syrupy mud.

"What can I do for you?" asked Lord Bannister, polite even in his despair. The girl looked with dazed eyes at the wrecked state-room but scarcely seemed to notice the havoc for which she was responsible.

"I... I wonder," she said, "if you'd mind if I stay in here for the rest of the crossing? We'll be there soon, anyway... I am being followed."

"Perhaps you would allow me to escort you back to your state-room?"

"Oh, no! By no means! I mustn't let you leave your room... I couldn't have you run into trouble... on my account! There is a murderer lying in wait for me! One of them just served a sentence of six years... Oh, I'm sorry... I... I think I'd better go away after all..." And she began to move towards the door.

Then at last the eminent scientist observed that the girl was shaking like a leaf. He could not let her go; he took her hand and found it cold as ice.

"Please sit down. First, you must have a spot of whisky." When she was sitting in Lord Bannister's comfortable chair with an empty glass in her hand the girl in the heliotrope pyjamas felt considerably less uneasy. Lord Bannister's alarm, on the other hand, was increasing every minute.

"I don't think... this is quite in order, you know," he began, for the awful impropriety of the situation was beginning to weigh upon his mind.

"But I am being followed by a murderer... He is waiting outside this room," Evelyn stammered. "I daren't even go as far as my cabin."

"But you can't stay in my state-room all night in your pyjamas... That wouldn't do your reputation much good. And besides, I have strong views about what is morally permissible."

"You are right, Lord Bannister," she whispered bravely and started for the door; but she presented such a pitiful sight that the scientist once again barred her way.

"I can't let you go away like that." He walked up and down nervously, jingling a few coins in his pocket as he struggled with the question of what was morally permissible. "There's nothing wrong, I suppose, in your spending a few hours with a physician when you are in such a state of nervous agitation. Sit down, please. It will soon be daybreak and then we will be arriving at Calais." He had been speaking in his most formal and scientific tones and so he added in a more friendly manner: "I am sorry to seem so nervous... You mustn't take it amiss... After all, you can't expect to walk in and out of a man's state-room as if it were a pub."

He was rather annoyed. Without more ado, he seated himself at the table, picked up his book and began to read. Evelyn was overcome with shame and sat watching him sadly. Then she knelt on the rug and began to pick up the pieces of broken glass. Lord Bannister could not resist a sidelong glance at her as she worked nor could he reject the thought that she certainly looked like a lady, though there could be little doubt that she was an adventuress—or worse.

"Don't trouble yourself," he said. "The steward will clear all that away in the morning."

"I am really awfully sorry..."

"Please. We must dismiss this catastrophe from our minds. It can't be helped now. This couple of hours will pass, and I hope there'll be no gossiping... That would be exceedingly unpleasant... By the way, Miss Weston, just *why* are you being followed, may I ask?"

"I am looking for an old family jewel. And I'm being followed by a murderer who has accidentally discovered where the jewel has been hidden."

"Then I am very sorry for you. Generally speaking, I can feel only pity for people who waste energy and emotion on transient pleasures and vanities of this world. Money, family jewels... If you had studied philosophy, Miss Weston, you would be acquainted with Aristotle's maxim 'That which is not eternal is not true'."

"I *have* studied philosophy, Lord Bannister, and I am afraid that maxim was formulated, so far as I know, not by Aristotle, but by Hermes Trismegistos."

There was a painful pause. Lord Bannister was assailed by doubt and the unhappy conviction that he was not in a position to argue. His suffering was acute and his reply correspondingly frigid.

"This is hardly the time for a scholarly discussion. I am not under the impression that it is for such a purpose that I am entertaining you."

He pored over his book anew. A gentleman may have a duty to rescue damsels in distress—even damsels who only *claim* to be in distress. But he is not called upon to converse with them—especially if they have the temerity to correct a fellow's quotations, and still less if they have the impertinence to be right. He looked so severe that Evelyn became thoroughly alarmed. She sat down in an arm-chair behind him and said not another word.

The scientist seemed to be absorbed in his book but in fact he was not reading. He felt angry with the woman. For the second time his peace had been shattered by this blonde whirlwind. For the second time he had felt the shock of her lightning appearance. He didn't care for women who rushed upon him like a hurricane.

Yes, a hurricane was just the word for her! He had experienced the sultry calm before the storm when the tropical leaves stir lazily and the air is still and tense with heat;

and he had experienced the shock of the ensuing hurricane.

What mischief was she brewing now? But the minutes passed, there was no sound from behind his back and it was gradually borne in upon him that he was being a little too severe with this scholarly whirlwind. He began to wonder if he had really frightened her and to suspect that she was in silent tears.

He looked round intending to give her a friendly word, and found his visitor—fast asleep.

She was sleeping with parted lips, her head cradled in the corner of the big chair—like a child.

He was obliged to admit that the girl looked very pretty in that charming child-like pose. He even murmured this thought aloud, then went on with his reading, looking up from time to time to cast an uneasy sidelong glance at Evelyn. But she slept as only the young can sleep.

•3•

For the next hour and a half Evelyn slept uninterruptedly, while Lord Bannister continued to read—with a good many interruptions. With the first light of dawn Lord Bannister grew restless. They would soon be at Calais. It was time to get her back to her cabin before the other passengers woke up and began to move about the ship.

"Miss Weston."

She started up in alarm. Then as she took in her strange surroundings and realised the awful impropriety of her situation she began to blush with shame. Her nerves must have been frayed indeed for her to have felt such an unreasonable fear of Gordon that she had not hesitated to seek shelter in this unseemly fashion. She began to apologise again.

"Oh, I am so frightfully sorry. I apologise..."

"I have no illusions about the nervous system of the Modern Woman," he answered, with a slight gesture of deprecation. "Now make haste to your cabin and don't let anyone catch a glimpse of you on the way."

He opened the door for her and stood beside her in the passage. And it was there that Fate now dealt him her unkindest blow. It was a blow timed with devilish cunning and aimed with the precision of a well-rehearsed actor. For Evelyn and her reluctant host now found themselves face to face with the mayor, his garrulous helpmate and P. J. Holler, a trio of nature-lovers all waiting to catch a glimpse of the rising sun. But no sunrise could have pleased them more than the appearance of Lord Bannister and his charming young companion in her heliotrope pyjamas. The scientist's stern face betrayed none of the anxious thoughts which now invaded his mind. He preserved a dignified silence broken at last by the mayor.

"*Ah, vous voilà, milord!*" he cried. "You too come to see ze rizing of ze sun. And, I am happy to observe that Lady Bannister also is an admirer of ze nature!"

Meanwhile Pest Holler had already taken advantage of the first rays of the sun to photograph the embarrassed couple and now had the effrontery to come up to them and introduce himself.

"I am sure glad to meet you, Lady Bannister! P. J. Holler, of Provincial Papers, at your service, ma'am!"

The mayor, too, made so bold as to introduce himself and then presented his burbling wife. Never for a moment did it occur to them that the lady who had emerged from the scientist's state-room could be anyone other than Lady Bannister. Evelyn did not dare to speak and Lord Bannister could only produce a few inarticulate murmurs. By the time they recovered their composure, the trio had moved tactfully away, belatedly aware, as they now realised, that Lady Bannister could not have enjoyed being interviewed in her pyjamas. The mayoress became voluble in her reproaches; she was shocked by her husband's effrontery.

Left to themselves, Evelyn was apologising all over again. "Oh dear, what have I done? What have I done now," she moaned.

"My dear Miss Weston, you are something of a hurricane, only more dangerous. Don't you realise what you have done? I have just divorced my wife without incurring any publicity. And these people are now convinced that you are my wife. We shall have to make them realise their mistake immediately..."

"But Lord Bannister! What will they think of me? And what will they think of you? I hope I am speaking to a gentleman and that you are aware that it is your duty to guard my reputation?"

"I am sorry, Miss Weston, I have no intention of marrying again."

"I am not thinking of anything so drastic. It will be quite enough to put matters right if we leave the boat together at Calais. We must be nearly there now. In the meantime they may as well go on believing that I am your wife. You can thus keep the secret of your divorce. As soon as we have landed and your friends have departed I shall thank you for your chivalrous conduct and promise that you will not see me again."

"Your hand on it," agreed the noble scientist.

Miss Weston's ingenuity thus reduced Lord Bannister's public ordeal to those few moments when together they said their good-byes to the press magnate, the mayor and his wife, who, however, insisted on miladying Evelyn so much that it was the scientist's turn to blush with shame. Their own moment of parting came at last. The splendid Alfa-Romeo, which Lord Bannister had bought only a few days previously, was hoisted to the quayside; Evelyn told the porter to take her luggage to the express for Paris. Then they said good-bye to each other.

"Thank you very much indeed... and I'm very sorry," she said.

Then, slowly and sadly, she walked away.

Lord Bannister gazed after her, wondering not a little. She was an unusual girl, he decided, and really very charming. He almost missed her... even though she had made such a mess of his future. He would have to rack his brain for some lie to explain why his wife was not with him in Paris. Lord Bannister hated lies—first of all because he thought they were the cause of much inconvenience, and as we know, he had a distinct preference for peace and quiet. All the same, she was rather nice... And he saw her in his mind's eye as she was sleeping—parted lips, head on one side; like a child.

·4·

Evelyn huddled sorrowfully in a corner of the Pullman. She had been with the scientist for only a few hours, but during that time she had acquired a sense of security; she had been a damsel in distress and she had been rescued by a man. Now once more she was on her own.

There were few passengers on the train, and she had managed to find a seat in an empty compartment. A cheerful countryside rushed past the window; meadows and copses were regularly followed by wayside stations which her train saluted with curt whistles.

The compartment door swung open.

"May I come in?"

The man who entered was tall, bald-headed, and there was a disfiguring scar on his nose.

But the ex-convict no longer filled Evelyn with terror. Her panic during the previous night had been the result of extreme fatigue; she was no coward and though she quailed a little, she remained calm.

She nodded curtly in answer to his question thus indicating that she had no desire to enter into conversation with the man. Pointedly, she continued to look out of the window.

A few goats were nibbling at the sparse tussocks of grass on the embankment.

"You are making a big mistake, Miss Weston. It's bad policy not to have a chat with me. It would pay you to get to know the other folks in the game."

"I have no need to get to know you," she replied coolly, "since I know you already. You are Charles Gordon, recently released from Dartmoor Prison, and are now making an attempt to steal the late Jimmy Hogan's legacy. That's what you mean by 'the game,' I take it."

The crook smiled.

"If it was in fact my intention to steal the Buddha, I should take good care to avoid you. Why, if it should happen to be stolen I would be the first person you would suspect and you'd certainly run to the police with my description."

She had to admit that what he said made sound sense.

"What is it you want, then?"

He produced a cigarette-case.

"Do you mind if I smoke?"

"Not at all."

"I propose that we come to terms. With all my experience and ingenuity at your disposal you would have a much better chance of finding the statuette than you would by yourself. For, naturally, you won't be able to get hold of the diamond by wholly lawful means. The diamond is your lawful property, it is true; and there's nothing illegal about your attempt to gain possession of it. But first you have to gain possession of something that does not belong to you—the statuette. I don't suppose you would want the owner of the Buddha to know your little secret, so the only thing you can do is to steal it. And for such an enterprise, I may say without immodesty that, as a felon and criminal, I have an outstanding record of achievement for which Scotland Yard could provide me with excellent references. It would be childish of you—to put it mildly—to turn down my offer, which I'd consider, of course, on a fifty per cent basis."

"If I understand you right, you want to enter into partnership with me."

"That's right."

"Can I speak plainly with you?"

"Delicacy of feeling is something that can always be dispensed with in my profession."

"Right. Then you can take it from me that there is in this world no diamond beautiful enough, and no bequest substantial enough, to induce me to enter into partnership with a rascal."

The ex-convict looked out of the window, lost in thought, and took a few deep pulls at his cigarette.

"I didn't know that you were a woman of such strict principles."

"Now you know."

"There is yet another aspect of this matter which you may care to consider. Naturally, I want to get hold of the statuette whether you help me or not. And I am not in any position to pick and choose my method. I may have to rob you, knock you out, or even murder you. After all, if we fail to come to an agreement, I shall not be bound by the ordinary decencies, or any notions about fair play."

"No, probably you won't. And now that we know where we stand in this matter, you will be good enough to find yourself a seat in some other compartment."

"Let me tell you just one more thing."

An unpleasantly mauve tint began to suffuse the brow of the ex-convict.

"Do you seriously believe you have the ghost of a chance against me?" he shouted. "Why, you can see that

I'm already just as far advanced on the trail as you are and I haven't even seen the ledger."

"Yes, because you've been following me."

"And I shall continue to follow you."

Evelyn shrugged her shoulders.

"Sooner or later, I hope I shall find a way of throwing you off the scent. But if I don't, you can have the diamond for yourself." She moved as if to get up. "Do you wish me to pull the communication cord?"

"No, I'm going now. But I warn you that you'd be wise to hand over the sales ledger you've got in your suitcase." He did not explain that he had noticed the ledger when she had opened her luggage in the customs shed. The ledger was in her small yellow leather trunk. "I'll go half and half with you, if you let me see it..."

"I shall now count three and if you've not gone then, I shall pull the cord."

Gordon rose quickly and nodded.

"See you again."

"One... Two..."

The compartment door closed behind him.

Gordon retreated to a distant third-class compartment where his friends were waiting for him. For this venture he had taken two old cronies into partnership and they were all travelling together.

"She's digging her toes in," Gordon reported to Crony No.1. "As arranged, then, Rainer."

Rainer, a sad-looking, grey-haired gentleman wearing pince-nez who might have passed for a commercial traveller but was in fact a specialist in robbery with violence, responded in rather peevish tones.

"All right, all right," he said. "I'll see about it. Have you got this morning's paper by any chance?"

•5•

Evelyn was in fact less composed than she appeared. It was all too probable that her own chance of success was slight in an undertaking in which she was opposed by Charles Gordon with his excellent references for robbery with violence.

But what was she to do? She wanted to secure her rightful possession but surely it would be unpardonable to enlist the help of a man with a criminal record? She shuddered at the thought of working with a murderer. What was it Uncle Marius used to say? "Integrity is like the fee for a Gentleman's Tailor—not to be bargained over."

Well, she thought, let the future look after itself! She would fight single-handed.

She could always go to the police; and she might even come across a gentleman to protect her in her hour of need. If not, poverty might be her lot once more.

In any case, what *could* they do to her, she wondered, scornfully.

She received an answer to this question when the train arrived at Paris. There, a short, grey-haired porter seized her small yellow leather trunk and dashed away towards the exit, and Evelyn went on standing beside her second trunk, waiting for the porter to return.

But the minutes passed and the porter did not return. In fact Evelyn did not see him again, nor her yellow trunk containing the sales ledger. Had Evelyn travelled third-class she would have realised that the grey-haired luggage porter and Rainer were one and the same person. Just before the train drew into Paris the respectable-looking murderer had transformed his appearance by donning the peaked cap and tunic of a French porter.

"What a lucky thing," Evelyn was ruminating, "that I tore the vital page out of the book and stowed it away in my writing-pad in the big trunk!"

Gordon's reaction was much less philosophical when, after carefully thumbing through the ledger a number of times, it dawned upon him that the entry for which he was looking had been torn out and that Miss Weston had outwitted him.

"What I don't understand," said Rainer, after watching Gordon beat his head with both fists for several minutes, "is why you are so jumpy. We'll have to go on following her, that's all. Sooner or later we'll find out who she's looking for in Paris. And then we'll know who has the diamond."

"You're an optimist, aren't you. How do you know she won't fool us again?"

"I have an idea she won't. At the moment, we've put Beefy on her trail. Perhaps after her next move, we shan't even need the address, which we would already know if only you had been released a few hours earlier. That's the great drawback to life in jail: you can't leave it just when you choose. I say, where're you going to have lunch?"

Rainer's trick of suddenly firing trivial question at a fellow without warning tended to send Gordon's blood pressure soaring.

"I'm not going to lunch anywhere, thank you. I'm fed up to the teeth already!"

"In that case I can recommend coffee, at the Café Rome. But you must go upstairs—it's a Turkish woman who makes the coffee there... Hullo! What's the idea?"

A bulky volume had whizzed past Rainer's head.

After lunch, they were rung up by Beefy at the Café Rome.

"She has taken forty different vehicles so far," Beefy reported. "It looks as if she knows she's being followed and she's up to every kind of trick to put us off the scent. Much good it did her. First she called at 7, Rue Mazarin, and from there she went to 12, Rue Salpêtrière to see the manager of Columbus Travel Agency. She is still there now. I am speaking from a call-box across the street; I'm bound to see her from here when she comes out and I'll keep on her tail. Tell Gordon that at 7, Rue Mazarin, she inquired after a Mrs. Brandon, a widow, and was told that the flat was occupied by Edward Wilmington, the manager of the Columbus Agency. Either he's got the statuette or he can supply a clue. Perhaps it'd be a good idea if Gordon went to see this fellow Wilmington and ask him point blank if he's got the statuette."

"Right-o. I'll tell Gordon all. He'll be here any minute."

"Well, I must go. She's coming out now."

"Hallo!.. Wait..."

"What d'you want?"

"Do you know if there's any racing on today?"

Without a word, Beefy hung up.

•6•

At 7, Rue Mazarin, Evelyn obtained discouraging information. Lieutenant-Commander Brandon's mother had died six months previously. Soon afterwards, her daughter, Mrs. Wilmington, had died too. Since then, Mr. Wilmington had been in sole occupation of the flat. An unlucky sort of man, people said, to have lost mother-in-law and wife within such a short time.

Evelyn tried to lose herself in the crowds, travelling short distances in one vehicle after another. She looked back several times, but could not see Gordon. She decided that she had successfully evaded him.

But she was wrong.

Beefy had been dogging her all time. However many times she looked back, he always made sure that she didn't see him. She noticed a rather flashy, monocled gentleman on the opposite pavement and watched him smiling at a little girl whose ball he had kindly retrieved from the gutter. He was a stupid looking muscular gentleman but Evelyn never guessed that he was Beefy who owed his nickname to the fact that he had more brawn than brain.

From Rue Mazarin, Evelyn hurried to the Columbus Travel Agency and before long she was sitting in Mr. Wilmington's office.

The manager was a slim, well-dressed gentleman with greying hair, penetrating blue eyes and a youthful complexion. So this was the brother-in-law of the unfortunate Lieutenant-Commander Brandon and, very likely, the owner of the £ 1,000,000 statuette.

"My name is Evelyn Weston."

"What can I do for you, Miss Weston?"

"I am looking for an old family relic. It is a small, rather ornate casket surmounted by a ceramic statuette representing Buddha with head bowed."

"I know that statuette."

"I understand that it was purchased by Commander Brandon fifteen years ago, and passed subsequently into the possession of Mrs. Brandon, who died recently..."

"Oh, I think I know what you are looking for. That ceramic statuette must be among the works of art left by my late mother-in-law. She was very fond of that kind of thing. Now all her belongings are in my flat."

Evelyn spoke hesitatingly, for she was excited now and began to breathe quickly.

"Yes, yes," she said. "I would like to buy that statuette... It's an old family..."

"I'm sorry, Miss Weston, I'm afraid I can't sell anything left to me by my late mother-in-law."

"So you have got the statuette of Buddha?"

"My late mother-in-law was fond of *objets d'art* and has left a great many ornaments of one kind and another. I am attached to all such family relics and nothing would induce me to part with any of them. That sort of thing is not done in the best English families."

"I understand those things were the property of Commander Brandon..."

"I would be still more unwilling to revive unhappy memories of my unfortunate brother-in-law. No, I'm sorry, neither the Buddha nor any other of our family possessions is for sale." At this point, Mr. Wilmington was called to the telephone and she heard him arrange an appointment with somebody for that evening and then direct his secretary to order cold supper for two from Félix Potain. When he turned back to Evelyn, he refused her request in no uncertain terms. Thus she was unable to ascertain whether Wilmington was indeed in possession of the statuette of Buddha.

However, it seemed likely that the statuette, if it was still, whole, was to be found in Wilmington's apartment.

She was in very low spirits when she emerged into the street. Here she was thwarted and helpless, yet with the goal in sight. She would not yet resign herself to failure! She would persist in hoping for help from some quarter however unlikely, from old Hogan's ghost maybe, or, even more improbably, her own impractical, scholarly brain. She was determined to find a way of getting into Wilmington's flat. She would break into the house!

Evelyn shuddered, more from determination than horror.

From the next call-box she rang up Félix Potain.

"This is Mr. Wilmington's secretary, of the Columbus Travel Agency. Some minutes ago, I ordered supper for two for Mr. Wilmington and a friend... That's right... 7, Rue Mazarin... Would you please cancel the order?... Yes, probably tomorrow... Thank you..."

She hung up.

Through the glass-panes of the call-box, she eyed the man idling across the street. He was short, stout, showily dressed, wearing a monocle... This was the third time she had noticed him today... Only a little while ago she had watched him return a ball to a child in Rue Mazarin...

Her scholarly brain quickly informed her that the man had been following her. How could she have been so deceived! She should have realised that Gordon would choose someone she had never seen before to follow her. Well, she knew him now and she must get rid of him without more ado.

She emerged from the call-box and walked straight ahead, pretending not to have noticed Beefy. At the corner of the street, she hailed a cab and gave the driver the address of her hotel. Presently, peering cautiously through the rear window of the cab, she could see that a car was following close behind. Undoubtedly the dressed up lump of beef was within. She leaned forward to the driver.

"Monsieur," she said. "Here is ten francs for you... There is a man following me in taxi; he is pestering me. Will you please turn into the next street and brake just long enough for me to jump out. Then follow a zigzag route for a while to make the man think I'm still here trying to get away from him."

The driver grinned and took the money. He turned into the next street, cleverly drew up for a brief second so that Evelyn could descend, and sped on his way again. Evelyn sheltered in a doorway, and watched the second taxi with Beefy in it, hurtle round the corner in hot pursuit. And Evelyn's kind-hearted driver certainly took him for a ride. It occurred to him that here was a good opportunity to have some minor repairs done at a cheap garage in the suburbs, and so he drove right out of town, with Beefy on his tail, and didn't stop until he was outside the *Gate of Vincennes,* at the garage near the famous Père Lachaise Cemetry.

By this time Beefy had guessed that something was amiss. He got out, paid off his taxi, and hurried across to the other cab. All his fears were justified; it was unoccupied.

"Where is the lady you've been carrying?" he asked the driver.

"She's not in the cab."

"Not in the cab?"

"Well, go and take a closer look. Maybe she's hiding under the seat."

"Are you trying to play jokes with me?"

"Perhaps I am—for the moment," said the driver with a sinister look, tossing a heavy spanner in the air as if it was an Indian hatchet. Beefy enjoyed a fight, and would have looked upon one now as a case of justifiable self-defence; but he realised that that was no way to obtain information and therefore decided not to take offence.

"Look here, my man. Here's ten francs for you."

The driver lowered the spanner, swinging it loosely in one hand—a weapon no longer.

"Now where did you drop that lady?"

"When I drove from the Quay into the Boul' Mich. I slowed down and she jumped out. She said you were pestering her, and I believed her."

"And what do you believe now that you've seen me?"

"Now I'm sure that you were."

Beefy had obtained all the information he needed, and so he decided to give the driver a good trouncing. After all, a blow administered in self-defence was equally justifiable if given after a period of reflection. He therefore wrenched the spanner from the driver's hand, tossed it away, and proceeded to pummel the fellow for a couple of minutes, holding the man by the neck and pinioning him against the wall, taking care to keep as far away as possible so as not to soil his gaudy clothes. Since he could scarcely do himself justice with only one arm, he directed a few random kicks at the cabbie's knees.

The white-headed proprietor of the garage rolled an oil drum to a safe distance from the fray, and sat down on it, thus securing for himself a ring-side seat, as it were, from which to watch Beefy at his exercises. The display lasted for several minutes, after which Beefy let go of the battered driver and with two fingers flicked a speck of dust from his sleeve.

"Do you still think that I was pestering the lady?"

The cabbie staunched his wounds.

"Ahem... Now that I come to look more closely I see that you are really a very respectable gentleman."

"Good. Now take me to the Café Rome."

The boss relinquished the oil drum and quietly filled up the taxi with petrol while the driver settled himself once again at the wheel. Then he slammed the door and the taxi drove off, bearing the monocled gentleman to the centre of the city.

Beefy rushed into the café, greatly agitated, and discovered Rainer, the specialist in robbery-with-violence, playing chess with a knock-out specialist. Rainer excused himself and moved aside to hear his colleague's apologetic story of pursuit and failure.

"It's an odd thing," he ruminated. "Gordon had a sort of presentiment that she'd turn out to be brainier than you. It's my opinion that she's no newcomer to the game or else it's you that are getting old. Time spares no man, it seems, not even the gentlest of crooks. Gordon has gone round to that Columbus Agency you were speaking of on the phone. We are to wait here for him to come back. That's the programme."

"Who would have thought that she was such a sneak?" Beefy lamented.

"Certainly she behaved rather tactlessly towards a *bona fide* criminal. That's true. Tell me, how much does a cabbie charge you for a ride as far as Père Lachaise nowadays?"

At this moment Gordon returned, apparently in a state of great agitation.

"Where's the girl?"

"Well, ... er," Beefy stammered. "Well, she's given me the slip. Jumped out of a cab."

Gordon gnashed his teeth and swore.

"You damn fool! Now off you go and find Lord Bannister. It's on the cards that he'll be meeting her. He's taken a room at the Ritz. He may quite likely lead us to the girl. Send any messages back to this place. Rainer, you are to stay here and act as liaison. I must be on my way now."

"Where are you going?"

"To get the Buddha. It's in the flat at 7, Rue Mazarin."

"You ought to have a coffee first," said Rainer seriously, but Gordon merely gave him a withering look.

•7•

Once she had thrown off her "shadow", Evelyn walked back to the Quay. She paused outside a small draper's shop and studied the garments displayed in the window, then she went in.

"I want a black parlourmaid's dress and a frilled apron to go with it, like the one in the window."

She tried the dress on and left the shop still wearing it, her own dress rolled up under her arm. Next she bought a black leather bag into which she put her folded dress. Thus prepared, she set out to look for the nearest branch of Félix Potain's chain of delicatessen stores. Paris is studded with Félix Potain's stores. At Potain's she bought a selection of cold dishes, had them wrapped, and took her parcels to 7, Rue Mazarin where she rang the bell of Wilmington's flat. The door was opened by the charwoman.

"I am from Félix Potain's. I've brought supper."

"Oh, yes, I know," the cleaning woman muttered. "Will you just put it down."

"If you don't mind I'll lay the table and arrange the dishes. A supper from Potain's has to be served properly, you know."

"All right. Please yourself."

Quickly and dexterously, she laid the table and arranged the dishes while the cleaning woman continued to potter about in one of the inner rooms. Nothing could have been better for Evelyn's purpose. She hurried out into the hall and slammed the door loudly; but she did not leave the flat. She remained in the hall hidden behind a large cupboard. The cleaning woman came shuffling out slowly, tried the doorhandle to make sure that the door was shut properly, then went back into the room. Half-an-hour passed. It was growing dark. Evelyn continued her motionless vigil and this time luck was on her side. The cleaning woman appeared once more but this time she was wearing an overcoat and hat, and was clutching a small bag and umbrella. "She must be only a daily," Evelyn thought happily, "and she's going home now." She guessed right and in another moment was in sole possession of the flat!

She went quickly into the drawing-room and switched on the light. She breathed quickly now, feeling both fearful and agitated. There were three glass cabinets in the drawing-room, all of them filled with *objets d'art*. She could not see the Buddha. The rooms opened one into the other and through the open door of the dining-room she could see right into the small drawing-room. As she looked, one of the windows was slowly opened from without and there appeared over the window-sill first, two large hands, then, a bald head below which she could make out the disfigured nose of the crook Gordon.

She stood rooted to the carpet with terror.

CHAPTER FOUR. *Eddy Rancing makes inquiries but only receives information about cadaveric lividity and outward signs of injury. His interest is not aroused. He makes the acquaintance of Frau Victoria, the Head Gardener's wife, and meets Mustard, a loose-living ruminant. A Karlsbad souvenir finds no takers. Whimsical Gürti is chastised. Eddy is trapped by a gnome; some time later he swims to the next village. All's bad, but ends well.*

•1•

Mügli is situated on the shore of the lake of Mügli and is famous in Switzerland as the most insignificant village in the Federation. It is never patronised by holiday-makers or tourists from abroad. It was to this place that Eddy took a bus in the hope of meeting Councillor Wollishoff.

He encountered no particular difficulties in the attempt. While he was taking dinner at the inn, the local citizenry stood patiently in an orderly queue outside the window, consumed with curiosity about the remarkable foreigner. In the circumstances, all Eddy had to do was to bestow a smile on the first kindly, honest and intelligent looking gentleman of mature years to enter the inn; Eddy immediately placed him as either the local magistrate or a naturalist, and in a matter of seconds he had made his first acquaintance. True, the man, whose name was Guggenheim, and who was a coroner, turned out to be merely a visitor, but that was no reason why Eddy should not obtain information from him.

"Do you know the local people, Herr Guggenheim?"

"Well... This is my district and so I know it pretty well. Last year, when we had an epidemic of typhoid fever, I worked here for a considerable time."

"Do you know Herr Wollishoff?"

"When did he die?"

"He is still alive—so far as I know."

"In that case I haven't had honour of meeting him. Generally speaking, it's only the dead that I meet in these parts. And of course the grocer. One of my in-laws. Apart from that, I don't go into society a great deal. You see, mine is an absorbing profession necessitating profound and concentrated study."

He launched into a glowing account of the coroner's generally maligned profession. He was no routine worker. He believed in his métier. He was sure that it was possible to put a great deal of individuality into the thing if you had a natural turn for it and adopted a critical approach, refusing to accept conventional patterns. Take cadaveric lividity...

"Some other time, my dear Herr Guggenheim. Some other time... For the moment, I should like first of all to meet Herr Wollishoff."

Eddy's obvious lack of interest momentarily damped Guggenheim's professional ardour and he refrained from going into details.

"I called at Wollishoff's place on one occasion though I have never met him personally. His caretaker died and I went to see the body; there were signs of injury and I decided to call in the police. Eventually his wife was arrested on suspicion and that was the last time I was in the house."

"And since then?"

"Since then she has been in jug, for the post-mortem revealed..."

"I think we ought to leave the dead to rest in peace."

"Agree! But only after we have examined them. My principle, sir, is this: to keep an open mind until after the autopsy. Last year, in St. Gall..."

Eddy Rancing did not stay to learn what had happened to Herr Guggenheim in St. Gall the previous year, although that gentleman seemed to find it even more exciting than the case of the injured caretaker. Eddy Rancing paid his bill and left.

·2·

Outside the inn, he began to consider possible excuses for calling on the assessor. He had not been reflecting two minutes when there appeared before him the nightmarish figure of a chambermaid. In normal circumstances the poor girl could have been no beauty and at this moment when one cheek was swollen to twice its size as a result of a poisoned tooth, she looked very like some evil spirit. She walked straight up to him.

"I am Victoria," said this apparition. "I'm Head Gardener Krüttikofer's wife."

"What can I do for you?"

"Herr Adalbert Wollishoff has sent me to tell you, sir, that he desires to speak to you, sir. But you'd better make sure that you shout good and hearty when you speak to *Herr Gewerberat,* because he's deaf, poor man. In the left ear. It's from the 'flu. Went under the knife, too, he did, last year."

Amazed, Eddy followed the swollen-cheeked female as she walked cautiously ahead in the darkness. At first, he thought she was being practical, but after he had stepped ankle-deep into a puddle for the fifth time he knew that Frau Vicky Krüttikofer's caution was due to her anxiety to keep her feet dry.

"Do you know why Herr Wollishoff has sent you for me?"

"What's happened..."

"I asked you," Eddy shouted nervously, "why your master has sent you for me."

"Oh. You see, Helli's not at home. She's gone to Erlenbach to fetch the papers. We take Zürich paper."

At the moment he stepped shin-deep into a puddle.

"You have to watch your step, sir. The road's wet," said Victoria unnecessarily. "It'll be paved with clinker bricks next year. They've already locked up two men for making off with the money. Now Hütrich's contracted for the work. He won't embezzle any, I'm sure, because he's had his share of jail already."

Eddy was now given a violent shove from behind which nearly dislocated his spine: it was a cow, which had tried to overtake them without due regard for traffic regulations.

"I told you to watch your step, sir... Mustard, you scamp!! She's a real bohemian, this animal! Comes home every evening and always uses the footpath."

"Where *is* the footpath?" asked Eddy despairingly. He rescued his hat from the mud into which it had been hurled by a friendly wag of the cow's tail.

At last they reached the house.

As he entered the old-fashioned dining-room, delightfully furnished with heavy oak furniture, the first thing that struck him was the number of cats of various sizes with which the room seemed to be inhabited; there was also a red-crested parrot perched on a swing above the dense foliage of an evergreen plant. Seated demurely in one armchair was a girl of indeterminate age but nearer forty than twenty, doing some kind of embroidery. A hawk-nosed old gentleman with a white beard and a head quite bald except for a few absurdly long hairs, advanced to meet him, leaning on a stick, but he collapsed straight into Eddy's arms, having stepped on the trailing girdle of his dressing-gown. For a few seconds, the old gentleman rested in the visitor's arms, exhausted.

"I've told them over and over again to cut some of it off... But no, they think that would spoil it! One day, I'll break my neck on it... Pleased to meet you."

"The honour is mine."

"Who has sent you?"

Eddy shouted:

"My name is Edward Rancing!"

They were now joined by the girl.

"My name is Grete," she said. "You have to speak loudly to father, as he is somewhat hard of hearing. Sit down, please."

He sat down. Fräulein Grete told Eddy that a dozen people had rushed to see them after hearing him inquire for Herr Wollishoff at the inn. Thereupon her father had of course immediately sent for him. It was not long before the Wollishoffs invited Eddy to stay with them for a few days; they sent for his luggage, prepared a room for him and begged him to wash and change before the evening meal.

After dinner, they all took part in a friendly bawling-match for the rest of the evening. The old man had lost his hearing aid two years before, but could not find it in his heart to buy a new one.

At last, about eleven o'clock, Eddy ventured to mention the purpose of his visit. By now, three cats were dozing peacefully on his lap.

"I come from London and I'm an art collector."

"What does he say?" old Wollishoff asked his daughter wheezily, for he was a victim of asthma.

"He's an art collector!" Fräulein Grete screamed.

The old man nodded his head sympathetically several times.

"I have a nephew who is an optician," he confided.

Meanwhile a few more visitors had arrived—the chemist, the theatre manager and a playwright, Herr Maxl, who had for several years been working on a drama entitled *William Tell* and who made a living as a professional visitor to those houses in which he enjoyed a reputation as a widely travelled man. It was true that he had once travelled as far as Brno, on behalf of a cattle dealer.

·3·

Later in the evening, Eddy drew Fräulein Grete aside. The girl had a small, pallid face reminiscent of a lemon. She wore a blue bow in her hair and when she smiled she looked like a newsreel version of a Japanese premier who has just handed in his resignation. She was exceedingly ugly and this was in no way mitigated by a set of false teeth.

"I collect the works of a number of English ceramic artists no longer living. Worthless stuff, as a matter of fact, but, you know, everybody has his little weakness."

"Ah, I know that. I have an aunt who is always washing her hands. She can't break herself of the habit. Can you tell me just what is the point of always washing one's hands?"

"As I way saying, I am an art collector..."

"But for heaven's sake, do tell me: what's the point of washing one's hands?"

Young Eddy had to restrain his fervent desire to aim a fast one at her citrus head.

"I am on the look-out for old pottery ornaments," he repeated faintly, much of his energy being employed in the inner conflict just mentioned. "I have consulted the sales ledger of one firm and discovered the names of people who bought some of the things I am particularly keen on. Seventeen years ago, Herr Wollishoff, your father, bought two pieces from Messrs. Longson & North, London."

"Those pieces were duly paid for!"

"No doubt they were. Quite so. That, however, is beside the point now. I am interested, among other things, in a piece called 'Harvesters'," he mentioned that piece on purpose, in an effort to make his inquiry less conspicuous, "Also in a case surmounted by a statuette called 'Dreaming Buddha'."

"Ah, I gave that away as a present a long while ago!"

The room swam before Eddy's eyes. He had to sit down. At the same moment he became aware of a shooting pain in one ankle. He had trodden on a cat which was now taking revenge.

"For shame, Gürti," said Grete in the namby-pamby tones she might have used to a baby. "She's so frightfully whimsical."

"You gave it away! Oh... Yes, whimsical. Rather."

"Yes, I gave it away. I never liked that 'Harvesters' piece."

Under the narcotic effect of his reviving hope, Eddy managed not to feel the persistent clawing of the cat.

"And what about the 'Dreaming Buddha'?"

"That's only worthless junk. I keep it in my bedroom. If you would like to see it I'll fetch it for you."

"If you don't mind. It'd be awfully nice of you."

The moment she was gone, the whimsical cat Gürti was sent flying along a graceful curve stretching from Eddy's foot to behind the *jardinière* of evergreens. A plaintive miaow interrupted the fireside vociferation of the local intelligentsia.

When Grete returned she held in her hands the statuette! The Buddha! He was represented sitting on the lid of a small enamelled case, head bowed in contemplation.

Eddy stretched out his hand and casually, not even looking at it, she handed it to him. In another moment he held the precious object in his hand!

The intelligentsia came over to admire it. Old Wollishoff, having in some obscure fashion gained the impression that Eddy too was deaf, shouted into the poor fellow's ear at the top of his voice.

"That's nothing! You ought to see the marble statue of Pestalozzi and his wife—on the plinth in Zürich Square!"

"Yes, that is a fine piece, to be sure," she said.

Eddy continued to hold in his hand the ceramic statuette containing the fabulous diamond. He had only to dash the little piece of pottery to the floor and he would be able to see it glint in the light of day. But then everyone else would see it too. He longed to run off with it without another word.

"Keep cool, Eddy," he told himself. "You must summon all your wits now and preserve your *sang-froid.*"

"This is not in the least valuable, but I am extremely fond of this sort of thing," he told Grete. "If you will let me have it I'll give you a very nice wrist-watch in exchange. I wouldn't offend you by offering you money."

"I wouldn't even give it away," she said. "It's my sewing-box." She opened the square box on which the statuette rested and revealed an assortment of sewing cottons, thimbles, a pair of small scissors, and needles. "Besides, this used to belong to Mama. It's a keepsake. I won't let you have this one. But if you buy me a wristwatch I'll let you have the Karlsbad cup. That's a very fine piece too, and we don't use it."

All Eddy's offers were of no avail. He begged, promised, cajoled, but he was only wasting his breath.

Eddy felt completely frustrated. Here he was, holding the Buddha in his hand and yet unable to secure it for himself. The diamond might be enclosed within the statuette but the statuette was as it were enclosed in the girl's obstinacy and protected by her hideous grin, which reminded him of a church gargoyle, and which, for all he knew, might even be a symptom of weak-mindedness. For the moment he had failed.

•4•

He now set himself to devise some other scheme.

It should not be too difficult. Police records inform us that it is possible to break into strong rooms, dynamite one's way through walls and prise open iron doors. It should therefore be a comparatively simple matter to get hold of a Hindu deity attached to a sewing-kit which was kept in the unlocked room of a deaf technical consultant's half-witted daughter.

Eddy decided that the simplest procedure would be to conceal himself in the lumber-room opposite the girl's room on the third floor, which he had observed when saying good night to her.

"Whose room is this?" he had asked her lightly.

"It's occupied by all kinds of old lumber," she had replied, laughing. "And our gardener keeps his Sunday Best in there, too."

Eddy opened the door of the lumber-room a little, and peered in. The gardener's leisure clothes were hanging near the door. Judging by that Sunday Best, the gardener must be the most down-at-heel citizen in the Federation. The lumber-room would be a very good place in which to hide, he decided.

Eddy wished his hostess good night and as soon as she had closed the door of her bedroom, dived into the lumber-room. He knew very well that in an hour's time, Grete would go downstairs again to fetch a supply of food from the larder. He had made this extraordinary observation the day before. At dinner, she had hardly touched the dishes, merely nibbling now and then like a little bird. But during the night, Eddy had had a headache and went out to take a turn in the garden; looking casually through the window of the drawing-room he had seen Grete sitting at the table with half a Bologna sausage and a fantastic pile of potato salad in front of her. She was eating so greedily that Eddy thought she must surely choke any minute.

This was the secret knowledge on which Eddy now based his plan of campaign. He would bide his time until she went downstairs and began to tuck in; then he would dive into her room, grab the Buddha and make a get-away with his prize. He was just pondering over the quickest way to leave the district, as he crouched in a battered bath-tub which, along with some garden tables and a chair with three legs, occupied the back of the lumber-room, when the gardener popped in to don his Sunday Best. Quietly the old fellow changed his clothes mumbling to himself all the time about a certain person who believed that a gardener was God who, if he wished, could make even a penny tulip bulb burst into bloom. The name of that certain person seemed to remind him of a number of rather insulting terms, which he solemnly uttered before hanging up his working clothes. Then he departed and—locked the door from the outside!

Now who could have imagined anyone locking a lumber-room?

For a second, as the sweat broke out on Eddy's brow, it seemed to the young man crouched in the bath-tub that the lumber-room had indeed turned into a bathroom. He clambered out of the bath and tried the door. It was certainly locked, and there was no window in the room. His first reaction to this imprisonment was to feel ravenous hunger and an overwhelming urge to ram the door with his head.

In impotent rage, he shook his raised fists at the ceiling as if blaming the sheets suspended there to dry. Then he kicked aside a garden gnome so that he could pace up and down.

When he discovered that he had left his matches downstairs, his rage knew no bounds and he almost chewed his cigarette-case to pieces. Next he caught his finger in a mousetrap. Some time later, he heard the girl steal out of her room on her surreptitious nocturnal raid of the larder, intent, no doubt, on gobbling up the remains of the Bologna and any potato salad that might have been left from the night before. When he sat down on a broken candlestick he nearly cried out with pain. He picked it up and hurled it at the head of the garden gnome he had just tossed out of his way.

Morning came at last. A key turned in the door, and the old gardener reappeared to put on his working clothes to save his precious Sunday Best. It was about five o'clock, still dark, and through the open door came the autumn smell of wet earth.

Suddenly, the gardener stopped in his tracks, puzzled. He stared in amazement at the majolica garden gnome on whose head he was in the habit of hanging his cap and saw that this had been replaced by a dilapidated cluster-candlestick. The gnome had moved since he saw it the previous evening! He looked at the grinning gnome as he puzzled out the mystery of the candlestick and slowly came to the conclusion that the lumber-room was occupied by someone other than himself.

At this stage he would undoubtedly have turned to flee, but before he could do so, the presence in the lumber-room of some other person was confirmed in no uncertain manner: a violent blow on the back of his head sent him sprawling among the exposed springs of an ancient relic of a couch and his head pierced the canvas of a picture depicting the family of bears which had given to the City of Berne its name.

The old man let out a yell which brought the kitchen boy, a box of floor-polish still in his hand, scurrying along the passage and into the lumber-room. Eddy leapt into the passage, collided with the kitchen boy and knocked him to the ground. And now, in the darkness, the kitchen boy joined the gardener in his cries for help.

The pyjama-clad figure of the door-keeper appeared at the bottom of the stairs. Eddy flung himself downstairs and at the eighth step from the bottom leapt upon the man. Together they crashed to the floor but Eddy was on his feet in no time, and dashed through the door. He raced down the drive into the early morning obscurity of the garden.

Thither he was pursued by the kitchen boy, still clutching his box of floor polish, the gardener, wearing his workaday clothes plus the conversation-piece depicting the ancestral namesake of the City of Berne and the pyjama-clad door-keeper. As dawn began to break, the cook, a superstitious woman, glimpsed at the strange carnival procession, and it was weeks before she got over the shock.

Suddenly, as luck would have it, the pursuers were favoured by the appearance of a hay waggon which effectively blocked the fugitive's path.

Unable to go forward, Eddy dived through the hedge and landed flat on his face on the other side of the ditch, only a few yards from his pursuers. He zigzagged his way among the trees, and suddenly found himself on the lake. Gently he lowered himself into the cold water. He took a deep breath, then dived and swam underwater as far as he could.

The pursuers therefore heard no splash and in the dim light of dawn, the sheet of water lay smooth before their eyes.

They turned and went back to the house.

Half an hour later, Eddy Rancing, exhausted, heaved himself ashore at Schwacht bei Zungli am See, a small town famous as the birthplace of two trade association chairmen.

It was daylight now and frogs were croaking happily in the reeds. But Eddy, blue with cold and dripping wet, sat down on a rock at Schwacht bei Zungli am See, and cried bitterly.

CHAPTER FIVE. *Evelyn is compelled to commit an indiscretion. There is draught, followed by gun-fight; in the end, a lot of people are run in in a police round-up. Everyone is being pursued as well as pursuing everyone else. The gangsters form a syndicate, then repair to The King of Beans. A banquet is spoilt by a tropical storm, and the person fêted leaves on a long motor tour, in full evening-dress.*

•1•

Evelyn scarcely dared to breathe lest she betray her presence in the flat.

In one of the rooms, a clock began to chime out the hour. The gangster climbed over the window-sill and stepped into the room. Then he carefully brushed his trousers to remove all traces of the lime which had soiled them as he climbed the wall. Evelyn watched his every movement, while Gordon remained ignorant of her presence.

She had withdrawn behind the door-curtain just in time and now couldn't help wondering what he would do if he discovered her. It was not an enviable situation to find oneself alone in a flat with a gangster. And she could scarcely cry out for help since she had no more right to be there than Gordon. They were both housebreakers in the eyes of the law.

She could hear the floor creak as he moved about. He must be going from one cabinet to the other, looking for the "Dreaming Buddha". She was filled with rage to think that it had been almost within her grasp and now she might have to actually watch her rival steal it while she stood by, afraid for her life.

Since she must now give up hope of gaining possession of the statuette she felt that she should at least try to escape or move to some more strategic position in which she could cry out for help.

Cautiously, she started for the widow. The thick carpet deadened the sound of her footsteps and the creaking of the floor. Now her hope of escaping depended on whether the handle would grate or not. She touched it, and very slowly began to turn it. Soundlessly the window opened. There was only a faint stir of air, probably because Gordon had left the window open in the adjoining room.

This time it seemed that Evelyn was in luck. The flat was on the fourth floor but there was a fire escape just beside the window. There was every possibility of escape.

But now that she felt secure of an avenue of escape, she plucked up more courage. She had not had time to examine the glass-case by the window and it was just possible that the little enamelled box with the Buddha was in it.

She moved a few steps back from the window.

Evening was closing in and it was dark in the room. She had to move quite close to the glass cabinet to make out the contents. At the very moment when she had satisfied herself that the Buddha was not there she heard someone slam the front door of the flat.

She heard first voices, then the click of the electric switch in the entrance hall.

Wilmington had come home, bringing a visitor with him!

•2•

"But he ordered supper for eight o'clock only," was Evelyn's first thought. Now she dared not move. The gangster, too, must be standing riveted to the floor as she was, and equally dismayed.

What now?

"Your attitude, Adams, absolutely beats me," she could hear the host saying firmly. "It was out of curiosity, not fear, that I yielded to your request to visit me in my flat."

"You'll understand everything soon enough," said the other shortly.

The door was ajar, and Evelyn was able to see quite clearly all that was happening in the dining-room. The visitor was a short, stout man, with a slightly rasping voice and a slovenly club-footed gait; a cigarette drooped from the corner of his lips and he allowed the ash to fall and rest on the front of his coat, making only the most perfunctory gesture of flicking it away. He had scarcely been in the flat for a minute when Evelyn became aware of the foul odour of cheap French tobacco.

Wilmington seemed both pale and nervous. She noticed an occasional twitch of his fine nostrils and he gnawed his lips as he paced the room. The stout one flung himself into an armchair, and, with the seemingly confident air of the bully and in similarly strident tones he began:

"Look here, Wilmington. You're expecting Fleury at eight o'clock; so you have just sixty minutes to consider my offer, because I'm not going to wait till our friend arrives. I must warn you that your game is up."

"You want to frighten me."

"No, I don't. This is only a warning. Four months ago, when I told you that I suspected you had Clayton's map, you laughed at me. You said you'd given up spying since your marriage; that you had nothing to do with that unhappy fellow Brandon's tragedy; and that I should leave you alone or you'd report me to the police. I knew you were only bluffing."

"You are bluffing yourself, Adams," the host said, with the gentleness of a purring leopard. He narrowed his eyes unpleasantly.

"I know your tricks—after all, we used to work together..."

"Then you ought to know that I carry a gun in the outer pocket of my coat, and that at the present moment my finger is on the trigger. And you must also have seen me pick a fellow off by firing from my pocket at a distance of fifteen yards."

Wilmington glared at the man in impotent rage.

The stout chap took out another Caporal with his yellow, claw-like fingers and lit it from the stump of the one he had just smoked. He stubbed out this stump on a glass salad-server, and from the expression on his face one would have thought he was in great pain.

"You've been holding out on the map in the hope of getting a higher price for it once the riots in the colonies had been quelled. What you forget is that these delaying tactics have given me time for making some careful investigation. Quite apart from my own formidable influence there is also to be considered the fact that my employers can use their authority all over the world. I have taken full advantage of my fortunate position and I am now here to take possession of the map together with the necessary documents before Fleury arrives here or, possibly, the police. For naturally we are all under police observation."

"My dear fellow, you are very confident in your game of bluff. But I know you of old."

"Since you are so insistent, I will now remind you of some of the facts which have put you in my power. When you realise just how familiar to me are your foul deeds, you will not be so ready to speak of my 'bluff'. Well, then my dear Wilmington—or should I say Mr. Stuck, since that was the name on the warrants when you were in the Intelligence—a year ago you married Lieutenant-Commander Brandon's sister. Your address and manner as well as the financial support you received from your employers made it possible for you to move in good society. As Brandon was a most capable man with an important post as ordnance officer in the Admiralty, your marriage gave you new scope in your work. And you didn't fritter your energies away. You did not go in for stealing merely trivial documents. You did not waste time on minor snippets of information. You were biding your time until something big came your way, meantime adapting yourself until you felt at home in your high-class surroundings. And since you are sly and cunning as well as clever you managed very well. At last came your lucky chance. Clayton, the explorer, returned from his last expedition, dangerously ill. He had been exploring the jungles of Central Africa and when he arrived in Britain he was a dying man. For several weeks the newspapers were full of his story and loud in praise of his achievements. Nevertheless, no more than a handful of people knew that the man had handed over the Minister of Defence a diary, several maps and a great many photographs. He had struck oil—oil wells of exceptional richness!"

Wilmington shrugged.

"I've already heard that story."

"Wait a minute...All this priceless material was placed in an official envelope at the Ministry of Defence, sealed in five places and delivered to the Admiralty's cartography department. In due course this envelope found its way to Lieutenant-Commander Brandon's desk. Soon afterwards, Clayton died. Now you are just as well aware as I am of the immense importance of a discovery of oil in African territory not yet controlled by any of the Great Powers! And no one working for the other Powers had managed to get anywhere near that particular territory. The orange-coloured envelope containing the map and relevant information was the only key to possession; never in all the history of espionage had there been such a priceless document. But the man who had access to it was himself unapproachable. Meanwhile riots had broken out in the colonies and all the Great Powers were united in opposition. It was at this moment that you gained possession of the orange-coloured envelope with the five seals!"

"Tell me, Adams, why don't you write? With your vivid imagination…"

"Because, as you will shortly have to admit, I'm more gifted in my old profession. Let me tell you that your life is at stake now; the police are looking for you, Fleury, Hannusen and everyone else involved."

"Will you kindly get to the point and tell me what you want?"

Adams lit another cigarette from the stump of his last one, then blew forth a huge cloud of smoke which rained flakes of ash on every side. He lay back still more comfortably, throwing his legs over the arms of his chair, and continued in drawling tones, but without ever taking his hand from his bulging coat pocket.

"In your endeavour to carry out your plan you corrupted a whole family. Today, only the eldest of the Brandon brothers and the unfortunate lieutenant-commander are alive—if any can be said to be alive after spending agonized months in the hell of the Sahara… Ah, you have gone pale? Didn't you know that Brandon was in the Legion?"

"Rubbish!" Wilmington hissed, and took a step forward.

"Be careful!" There was a threatening rasp in Adams's voice now. "My finger is still on the trigger."

The bulge in his pocket moved menacingly, and Wilmington, panting with rage, was checked. The stout fellow laughed.

"Beginning to find the story a bit awkward, are you? Your wife, Isabel Brandon, gave birth to a child. One day, the baby disappeared. You told the despairing mother that she could get her child back provided she obtained an impression of the office keys used by her brother, the naval officer! You taught that unhappy woman whom you had driven half-crazy with despair, how to take impressions like a burglar. She endured two weeks of mental agony, then produced the impressions. But how would it be possible for you to get hold of the document without losing your splendid social position? You devised a magnificent scheme. Lieutenant-Commander Brandon doted on his brother, a young man of twenty who was head over heels in love with a dancer. But that lady was your chosen instrument. I know her well. Ethel Ardfern is her name. She had seduced the boy, who had been brought up by Lieutenant-Commander Brandon since his father's death. She persuaded the boy, Derek, to run away to Canada taking her with him. The day they were to take a train to Southampton, the boy wrote a letter to his brother."

Wilmington stood riveted to his place and looked fixedly at his visitor.

"That letter read as follows. 'George, I've had no choice but to do this. Can you forgive your wicked brother?—Derek.' They agreed to post the letter immediately before embarking in Southampton. Ethel had a big car and before driving out to the railway station, she asked him to accompany her on a visit to her mother, who lived near London. But she stopped the car in a lonely country lane and a fellow called Dickman, who was her accomplice, murdered the boy. That night, Ethel danced at the bar as usual. But Derek's farewell letter, extracted from the boy's pocket, was by then on its way to you. The following morning, you stole the envelope—and your methods, I have to admit, were worthy of a genius. In the morning, you called at the Admiralty a few minutes before Lieutenant-Commander Brandon was due to arrive. By some means you managed to gain access to his office; there you used the duplicate key, extracted the document, and went back into the vestibule and sat down. When Brandon arrived you were waiting for him with his brother's farewell letter together with the wax impression used to make the duplicate key.

You told him that Derek had rung you up in a state of great agitation to tell you about some crime he said he had committed... He dared not ring up his brother... he was in dept... he would have landed in jail... he had been blackmailed and driven to have a duplicate key made that he could steal the orange-coloured envelope. Now he was emigrating, leaving England for good. Naturally—so you told Lieutenant-Commander Brandon—you had driven straight to Derek's rooms. The boy had already gone, leaving behind this letter and the wax impression. You hadn't been able to make head or tail of the business, so you'd brought the things round to Brandon. The Commander stared, pale-faced, at the impression and the letter, in which he read the lines, written in his younger brother's familiar hand: 'George, I've had no choice but to do this. Can you forgive your wicked brother?—Derek.' He then went into his study and found that the orange-coloured envelope containing Clayton's map had vanished. The poor blighter had not the faintest idea that the orange-coloured envelope, folded in two, was in the pocket of your overcoat at the moment hanging in the vestibule. Who would have thought of such a thing? It was truly a stroke of genius!"

Now Wilmington was no longer standing bolt upright. His eyes were fixed on the floor. Adams lit himself yet another Caporal from the wet, yellow stump, then poured himself some wine from a bottle on the table, and drained the glass.

"You had better luck with your scheme than you had dared to hope for. That crazy Brandon just could not bring himself to denounce his younger brother... He was not aware, of course, that he had been murdered... Well, so this mad hero, this Commander Brandon, decided to give his brother Derek a chance to make a fresh start; he did not want him to be a social outcast because of what he had done... Brandon wrote a letter to his superiors, telling them that the map had been stolen, that he felt responsible for its loss and therefore felt obliged to tender his resignation. He explained that he had taken the papers from the office without permission, and that on his way home he had been attacked and had his attaché case wrested from him.

"The authorities would not believe this story. Commander Brandon was denounced as a spy. They could not arrest him, but news of his disgrace circulated throughout the world. So you have ruined a respectable old family. The mother died here, in Paris. One of her sons was murdered, another had to flee the country, the eldest a misanthrope..."

"I've heard enough of your rot. How can you prove your extraordinary story?"

Adams grinned complacently.

"I can prove it all right. But I haven't finished my story yet. Some time afterwards, your wife died, too."

•3•

Wilmington had been pacing up and down, and when these last few words had been spoken he had his back turned to Adams. Now he swung round and stared at the stout little man in dismay.

"Ah, that one's struck a nerve, eh?... Well, let's the story straight. First I grilled Ethel Ardfern as I'd seen you do it. I got her on board a hired yacht...you get the idea? First inject with tetanus, then withhold inoculation until victim signs confession in the presence of witnesses. Ethel also knew about this kind of interrogation. She knew that no quarter would be given, and she spilled the beans to get the inoculation... Unfortunately, as she was a bit slow about making her confession, the inoculation didn't work..."

"You scoundrel!"

"Easy!" shrilled the stout fellow, pointing his gun at Wilmington's chest.

There was a moment's pause. Evelyn was paralysed with horror, her lips parted, her hands pressed to cheeks, in an unconsciously theatrical pose, while in the other room Gordon was also listening in amazement.

Wilmington sat down, lit a cigarette, and said nothing. White-faced, he drew deeply and blew out clouds of smoke.

"From Ethel's confession," Adams went on, "we learned of Dickman. He was the bloke that stabbed Derek Brandon to death. Dickman told us everything hoping that we would let him get away with it. Well, we didn't. I have him locked away on a boat in Toulon harbour, in spite of the fact that I have a written confession, duly witnessed, that he received his instruction and payment from you. I can also produce evidence to prove that your wife's death certificate was forged. Then I risked a heavy sentence some nights ago when I did a little exhumation on my own in Père Lachaise; your wife's body was examined by qualified experts who tell me that there is still the blue discoloration of cyanosis on her lips."

"Stop it!"... Shut up!... You..."

"I have more bluffs up my sleeve. For instance, we can easily get hold of Lieutenant-Commander Brandon. We've found out that he serves, under the assumed name of Münster, in the 2nd company of the Legion, and is at present being treated for serious wounds in Morocco. So, you see, my star witness is alive. The man whose name has been dragged through the mud because of your criminal activity is still alive!"

"Stop it, I tell you," said Wilmington, panting and cowering as if he had seen a ghost. "Take the map! Take it away! Only be quick about it, Fleury will be here any minute... How much are you prepared to pay for the orange-coloured envelope?... You have it, you bloody stool-pigeon."

"You won't do too badly. But first I want to make sure that the seals on the envelope haven't been tampered with. Don't try to tell me it's in the other room and don't put your hand in your pocket. Just go to the safe over there and open it."

Evelyn had been listening to the dialogue in a sort of coma. She was sure they would kill her if they discovered her presence. But terrified as she was, she could not put out of her mind the thought of the unhappy Brandons. She made a silent vow that if ever she got out of this place alive, she would make all these secrets public... Though it would be difficult to prove anything. Meantime Wilmington had crossed over to the safe from which he extracted a large envelope on which the five seals were evidently intact. He put it on the table and Evelyn had a great longing to snatch up the envelope and run off with it to Morocco to rescue poor Commander Brandon! She wondered if Gordon had also heard the story—or had he got away already? In any case, she would memorise the poor commander's alias as a legionary. Münster... Münster, she repeated to herself.

"We ought to move quickly now," Wilmington said. "Today, two different people came to my office inquiring after Commander Brandon. They pretended to be looking for a statuette of the Dreaming Buddha that was surmounted on some sort of a box—something left here with the rest of his belongings. I suppose that was just an excuse. They must have been agents from one of the organisations."

"Why? Isn't there a statuette like that among Brandon's things?"

"Oh, yes. I remember seeing it at the Brandon brothers' flat. In the bathroom, if my memory serves well. But I don't believe their story. They would have to think up something which would sound plausible. Somehow they must have found out that Commander Brandon did own a box like that."

Adams's face darkened.

"But why both of them ask the same question? It sounds to me as if there is really something about that statuette. A number of people must have discovered something special about it, the clues lead to you, and now they're all competing with each other to get there first. I don't like this business."

Wilmington paled.

"Do you think so? But what on earth would they want to with an enamelled case which has been in a bathroom for years—or with the statuette either, for that matter?"

The stout chap reflected.

"Have you got the statuette here?"

"Hell, no. I fobbed them off by saying that I had it, or at least that's what I let them think. The thing must be in Africa, with Brandon—though he may well have thrown away a gew-gaw like that when he absconded."

"I would give a lot to know about this Buddha business," Adams brooded.

"I say, Fleury may be here any moment."

"You're right. Now let's have that envelope."

"But you must hand over the money first, Adams! This represents two years of risky work by an ambitious man who has not yet received a cent for his pains."

"You have sacrificed enough lives in the cause for me to appreciate that fact."

At the moment there was the resounding crash of falling window followed by the tinkle of broken glass. A light breeze had arisen and a sudden gust of air had slammed the window in the room where Gordon was hiding. It was only because of the unusual stillness of the evening that this had not happened earlier.

·4·

Like two startled animals, Adams and Wilmington bounded into the next room. But Gordon was on the alert, and met them with a battery of chairs, one of which caught Adams on the shoulder. Next came a small table and a Chinese vase. Then Adams fired two random shots and hurled himself upon Gordon who retailed by seizing Wilmington by the waist, and tossing him bodily at his assailant. During the next few minutes the flat resounded with the noise of combat, the thud of falling bodies, the crash of overturned furniture and the splintering sound of broken china and glass; the general effect was like a stampede of beasts of prey.

Suddenly a shot rang out, fired from somewhere on the stairs outside the flat; this was followed by the sharp peal of the door bell and the sound of fists pounding on the door: next came the regular sound of a swinging axe. There was only a second before the door would give way; the police must have been lying in wait for Fleury and having caught him, were preparing to raid the flat.

In the empty room, the orange-coloured envelope with the five seals had been left lying on the table. Evelyn now saw her chance. She slipped into the dining-room, picked up the orange-coloured envelope from the table, put it in her handbag and stepped out of the drawing-room window onto the ladder of fire escape. Now she had all that was necessary to clear the name of the Brandon family and if she could find Brandon still alive he would surely be ready to give her the statuette in exchange for this envelope.

She was already planning to go to Morocco when the sound of fighting was redoubled and she realized that she was still in danger and might not even get to the street in safety.

Gordon hurled himself on Adams. Wilmington whipped out a gun. Now Gordon freed himself with a powerful kick that sent the stocky fellow rolling. He thus became a sitting target for Wilmington, who however did not shoot. The accumulated hatred, rage, resentment and thirst for revenge of a man whose vanity had been grievously wounded, welled up into a determination to shoot Adams like a mad dog. He fired into his face from a distance of only two yards.

But the gun misfired and it was Wilmington who now faced death, while Gordon escaped. For Adams heard the click of the trigger and aimed at Wilmington the bullet he had reserved for Gordon. Wilmington received it in the stomach, gasped, and with the last movement of his hand, clutched at the curtain, rolled over and wrapped himself into the bright brocade as if into his own shroud.

At that moment the door fell before the last blow of the axe and it was borne in upon Adams that Gordon had escaped and that he alone was left to face the police.

Quickly he ran into the dining-room, noticing immediately that the window of the adjoining room was wide open. Behind him he heard the commotion as the police surged into the hall, stumbling over the body of Fleury. He just had time to slam the door and lock it so that the police would be detained in the vestibule for a few more minutes. Then he leapt into the adjoining room, through the open window, and was standing on the ladder of the fire-escape in time to look up and see a foot lifted from the top step and disappear onto the roof. He fired a shot after the fugitive.

•5•

When she stepped out of the widow and looked down Evelyn cried out in horror.

In the street below, a pitched battle seemed to be in progress. Patrol cars were arriving, their sirens screening. People were running hither and thither and it seemed that

Rue Mazarin was being blocked on every side. Four men, handcuffed, their clothes in tatters, were led out of the house from which Evelyn was fleeing and were taken to a police van. In the light streaming from the open door she could see a man lying on his face, motionless, in a large, dark pool of blood. A smartly dressed woman was dragged by the straps of the handcuff fastened about her wrists, then hustled, screaming, into the van. This scene of horror was floodlit by the headlights of an armoured car.

When Evelyn heard the first shot fired in the flat behind her, she began to climb up the ladder, at first hesitatingly, then more quickly as she began to realize the danger of her situation. She could not flee in the direction of the street; her only way of escape was over the roof. She struggled upwards, tearing her skirt on the way, and summoned all her strength to grip the edge of the gutter and hoist herself onto the roof. Once there, oblivious of her bedraggled hair, muddy hands and torn clothes, she ran along the roof, searching for some place of safety. Once she fell to her knees and rested a moment in a pool of rain, almost unconscious with pain. She struggled to her feet, ran on and came to a halt beside a chimney-stack.

Then, looking back across her perilous route, she caught her breath in horror, for there, at the very point where she had emerged from the fire-escape onto the roof, she saw first two large hands, then a bald head and finally the nose with the disfiguring scar.

As she turned to flee once again from her enemy, the ex-convict, he was already so close that she could hear his footsteps. A shot rang out and she stumbled over some planks; a taut clothes-lone caught her by the throat; she fell, sprang to her feet and fled on.

There was another shot, but this time it was her pursuer who was being pursued: by someone who was himself being followed. She won a breathing space, for Gordon ran to cover behind a chimney and fired back at Adams. So they hunted each other while the Paris police hunted them both.

Evelyn seized the opportunity to run ahead, still clutching her small black handbag containing the valuable envelope, and suddenly she came to the sky-light of a studio.

Without hesitation, she gripped the frame of the open window, lowered herself into the room, hung there suspended for one breathless second, then, eyes closed, relinquished her hold.

Fortunately it was a rather low-ceilinged room, and she landed safely in the darkness within. She listened and began to distinguish voices in the adjoining room.

"You can choose which you like. The postcards are nine-by-twelve. But if you would like enlargements..."

She was in a photographer's studio.

Quickly, she looked about. There was a door on the right; this she opened, went through and crossed another dark room, this time long like an entrance-hall. When she opened a second door at the far end, she felt a rush of fresh air: she was on the stairs.

Hurriedly she descended, stumbling in her anxiety and again tearing her skirt. Her hands and face were sticky with mud but she had no time yet to worry about her appearance.

The stairs led down into a dimly lit yard. A servant girl was cleaning poultry; two white-aproned boys were emptying a large pail into the drain. Through an open door, she could see into a vast kitchen. This must be the yard of one of the elegant restaurants along the Quay. She made for the door of the building.

The police sirens were still wailing behind her but she thought that if she could only get through the restaurant she would leave the danger zone and reach the safety of the Quay.

One of the boys approached and began to look at her curiously. Her sense of danger renewed, she stepped boldly indoors, and walked straight through the kitchen without glancing at the dumbfounded kitchen boys; she opened another door—and found herself under the brilliant lights of an elegant restaurant. The diners sitting at the tables nearest to her raised their eyebrows in amazement for by now her clothes were in rags, her hair hanging over her shoulders and her face quite black with grime. She walked resolutely forward, intent on reaching the front door which, she could already see, gave onto the freedom of the Quay.

"Why, it is Lady Bannister! Good heavens, what have you been doing to yourself?"

It was the Mayor of Paris.

Seated next to the mayor was P. J. Holler, while at the head of the table Lord Bannister, in full evening dress, was presiding over what appeared to be a banquet attended by a very great number of very distinguished gentlemen.

•6•

Lot's wife, when she felt herself being transformed into a pillar of salt, could not have assumed a more vacant expression than that which appeared on his lordship's countenance when Evelyn made her astonishing appearance at the banquet held in his honour. For a moment, the silence was absolute. During that moment, Evelyn's brain was racing: she realized that Lord Bannister's reputation was at stake. The next moment, she saw in a flash the only possible way in which she could save the situation. She gave a little, embarrassed laugh and said, guessing wildly at the scientist's Christian name.

"Oh, Henry, I know I'm an awful nuisance, but I'm afraid I must ask you to take me back to the hotel immediately. Some clumsy cyclist has just knocked me down, here by the kerb. Look what's happened to my dress."

She knew on the instant that she had brought off her little *coup.*

The fresh tears and mud patches made what she said sound fairly plausible. The guests expressed their sympathy and spoke comfortingly to 'Lady Bannister'. One after the other, members of the Academy, university professors and generals introduced themselves, and 'her ladyship' said she was truly sorry she could not possibly stay with them in this state, and finally took Lord Bannister's arm and led him away.

As soon as they had settled themselves in Lord Bannister's car, Evelyn cautiously peered out to see if she had been recognized by her pursuers. She felt sure that so long as she had that envelope she could expect to be hard pressed by not a few desperate men. She could see no one. Lord Bannister waited patiently for her to turn round, then he said:

"Will you please shut the door and tell me where you would like me to take you?"

He was too indignant to say more. Indeed, he was too scandalized to be angry. It was true, and there was no use denying it, that several times in the last few days his thoughts had strayed in her direction and he had thought it would be nice to see her again. Nevertheless, he found the circumstances under which he now actually saw her, quite unnerving. He had to restrain an impulse to throw her out of the car. What on earth could this girl be doing? Why was she always to be seen in torn and muddy clothes? And what could she be up to that she had to prowl about the streets at night by herself?

It was just like her appear in this unexpected fashion, rushing madly towards him, her blonde hair glinting like lightning; for the second time she had descended on him like a hurricane.

"Oh, please drive as fast as you can and take me out of Paris, to some place quite out of the city where I can take a train or hire a car," she entreated him breathlessly.

"But… I can't do that in evening dress…"

"I'm being followed!"

"I seem to have heard you say that before. Now, my dear Miss Weston, I am fully aware of a gentleman's duty towards the fair sex; still, I must call your attention to the fact that, unfortunately, I am only a scientist, not a knight errant. I find it puzzling that, when we have such a well-qualified, efficient police force at our disposal, you should persistently seek *my* assistance. I have a great respect for you, Miss Weston, but perhaps you will allow me to repeat myself and point out that you have no right to walk in and out of my life as if I were a pub."

"You are right… I will get out at once," she said. But the next moment, she leaned against the windscreen and began to weep. She was afraid that every railway station in Paris would be watched—perhaps the garages, too. She knew that her life was in peril. Possibly they were already on her track and her only chance was to hire a car at some distant place outside Paris. She suddenly felt very lonely.

"Now please tell me where you want to be taken," said Lord Bannister resolutely, for he found it impossible to speak as curtly as he would have wished. "And kindly stop crying. I'll drive you out of Paris. I'll take you anywhere you want."

"To Marseilles," she said, her face brightening.

"What!" snorted Lord Bannister, for he had a strict regard for the conventions. "To Marseilles, in evening dress?"

"Oh, of course you mustn't do that. Just drive me a long way out of the city… to the nearest village where I can hire a car."

Angrily he trod on the accelerator, and the powerful Alfa-Romeo started noiselessly along the road to Lyons.

•7•

Meantime, on the rooftop the two men were still trying to conceal themselves, each one behind a separate chimney stack. Gradually the commotion in the street had subsided, and it would now have been risky to fire any more shots.

"I say, stranger!" Gordon called out. "Do you seriously insist on our tracking each other down? We're bound to be caught if we do." As the other made no reply, he added: "Much better to join forces. What d'you say?"

Adams made no reply.

"If we work together, we might find that girl with the document. I happen to have some information without which you can't hope to succeed. What I say is, let's team up."

"Who are you?"

"An Englishman. Of an allied trade."

"What use would I have for you?"

"You promise me equal shares in the deal with Clayton's map and I'll do the same for you in the deal with the statuette."

"What deal is that?"

"It's for a statuette worth one million pounds sterling."

"I suspected there was something fishy about that Buddha. Unfortunately, just now I've no time for anything except that orange-coloured envelope."

"Then we both want the same thing," Gordon replied. "We can get hold of the statuette *and* the envelope once we find Evelyn Weston. Well? Let's go halves. We could form a syndicate if you like. Or we could turn our backs to each other and get down from this roof separately. You, I suppose, don't want to grow a beard up here, any more than I do?"

There was a pause.

"All right," Adams said at last. "At the moment neither of us dare move from behind our chimneys. At least, I don't trust you. The best idea would be to meet at the King of Beans Tavern in half an hour. It's near the Château Rouge."

"All right. See you later."

Each man then retreated carefully from his respective chimney, covering himself as he did so.

As soon as he got down into the street, Gordon phoned Rainer.

"I want you and Beefy to come along to the King of Beans Tavern."

"Is the cooking good? I haven't had dinner yet."

"You damn fool! This is a matter of life and death. We may become millionaires if we can find Evelyn Weston."

"That's what you say! Beefy was on the phone just now saying that he saw her riding in Lord Bannister's car. They'd tanked up under his very nose on the road to Lyons. He's following them and will leave messages for us at every filling-station. I say, how far is that King of Beans place?"

•8•

Adams and his two men had been at the bistro some time when Rainer and Gordon arrived. The gentlemen introduced themselves, also their respective accomplices.

Yoko was one of Adam's confederates, a bearded fellow in a striped jersey who never stopped chewing tobacco and spitting. He had once been a contortionist in a circus, but had changed his profession after causing the death of more than one of his colleagues.

The other man with Adams was a Dr. Cournier, a hulking great fellow with a pale face, tired eyes and white hair who was a drug addict. He would make slow gestures with his bloated, freckled hands as he talked; he had a deep, reverberating voice and the kindly manner of a wise old man.

"Gentlemen," Gordon began, "we're pressed for time. There is in fact no necessity for me to collaborate with you; but if I don't, we are bound to clash at some point. And the cake is big enough to feed us all."

"To the point!" said the man with the beard, and he began to clean his nails with the tip of an incredibly long knife.

"Absolutely," declared Rainer. "It is high time we came to the point." He hailed a waiter: "Bring me fried veal, with plenty of chips, half a litre of claret, and two hard-boiled eggs."

"Well, then, gentlemen," Gordon went on. "I know where I can find the girl with the envelope. Also, I know how to get hold of the ceramic statuette worth one million pounds sterling."

"Now I know about that, too," said Adams. "That man Münster's got it. Still, if you tell us where the girl is, we'll agree to team up with you."

"We'll go fifty-fifty."

"It's a deal."

Gordon then supplied them with the bare facts of the case, beginning with the story of Dartmoor and Jimmy Hogan's will and ending up with Beefy's telephone message.

"It was lucky for us that Beefy lost track of the girl and so I was able to send him to tail Lord Bannister, in whose company Evelyn Weston had made the crossing posing as his wife. I thought she was bound to turn up again in his company. And sure enough, they met again, immediately after all that happened in Rue Mazarin."

Adams jumped to his feet.

"Then we'll run them down!" he cried turning to Rainer.

"When did you talk to your mate on the phone?"

"Less than an hour ago. The lousy service they have at this place! I've been waiting for the mustard for half an hour. No point in eating hard-boiled eggs without mustard."

The bearded man stopped trimming his nails and pointed the tip of his knife at Rainer's chest in a threatening way.

"Right. Get going, everybody!" Adams snapped.

Soon they were racing madly along the road to Lyons. At Armentières, they overtook Beefy in his taxi.

"They've outstripped me by a long way," he informed his friends when he had settled down in the Packard. "That scientist has a gem of a car. But he hasn't the faintest idea that we're hot on their heels."

The car raced along at breakneck speed.

CHAPTER SIX. *Reminiscences about a lighthouse and the Morse code. A fresh scheme founders four storeys up. The author of* Wilhelm Tell *takes possession of a gold-watch and has it valued at Högraben's. The fire-brigade is called out. Eddy Rancing quotes Shakespeare and Lübli the pipeman interprets. Eddy sends a telegram.*

·1·

Eddy wiped away his tears, untied a boat from its moorings and rowed back across the lake. He landed and made straight for his temporary home at Mügli am See, where the populace was still restive after the excitement of the early morning chase. Eddy waved from afar.

"I had him in my hands!" he shouted breathlessly as he approached the crowd. "As I was grappling with him we fell into the lake, and I'm afraid he was a stronger swimmer than me."

They gazed at the brave young Londoner with a mixture of respect and admiration.

"You are a hero," said Grete, giving him one of her eight-inch smiles. "I wasn't the least bit alarmed when I remembered that you were with us."

"I see you have sustained some outward signs of injury," said the coroner, joining them and taking a close look at Eddy's cracked lips. "Lips in that condition are usually excised for histological examination before the public hearing."

"Mr. Rancing," said the police inspector in the cool voice of authority. "Could you give us a description of the miscreant?"

"Certainly. A tall man with a small moustache. There were warts all over his face and a scar on his right arm-pit."

"Any unusual identifying mark?"

"His breath had a strong smell of liquor."

"Nothing unusual about that in these parts, I am afraid," said the inspector, lighting a pipe.

He hated pipe-smoking but felt that it was *de rigueur* for a detective.

"Any other particulars? Initials on shirt? Size of shoes? Strong physique, or weak?"

"I have seldom seen a more muscular burglar," Eddy said.

"I can assure you, the man is a Hercules."

"Good. We should be able to track the fellow down with the help of the Aliens Registration Office," declared the inspector confidently.

Eddy said he had no doubt they would. He hastened back to his room, where for the next twenty-five hours he remained in bed. He sneezed continuously and when, towards evening, Frau Victoria, Head Gardener Krüttikofer's wife, brought him a cup of herb-tea, he began to feel very ill indeed.

Eddy was not averse to an adventure, but he had really met with rather more obstacles than he had bargained for in this ghastly hole: it was enough to make even an Arsène Lupin long a quiet, settled life. Less than two years previously he had courted the daughter of the Dover lighthouse-keeper and had only been able to meet her on stormy nights when the duties of his office kept her father busy. Harrington, the hefty lighthouse-keeper, was a stern and forbidding parent, so that Eddy found himself obliged to learn to interpret the girl's signals in Morse. Between eight and nine o'clock every evening, the light in the small window of the light-house parlour would be switched on and off at regular, varied intervals. And on the shore Eddy, as efficient as any Sparks thanks to his sweetheart's coaching, would read the signals: "Dad...on eight-hour duty... Come... Gin running out... You dear..."

Thus had Eddy learned, for love, the art of telegraphy and of climbing lightning conductors. Such experiences had had a romantic flavour all their own. This Swiss adventure was something quite different: here, floor polish was hurled into his face by kitchen boys with pimply noses, people locked him into lumber-rooms, slapped his face and hustled him into cold lakes.

And yet he would have to do something about that Buddha. He lay in bed, convalescing, and plotting another line of attack. At last he conceived a truly brilliant idea; his own genius quite amazed him. In the afternoon, he went to see the local physician, Dr. Rüdiger.

"Glad to meet you, sir," the doctor said. "How do you do. And what brings you to see me?"

"I can get no sleep."

"I'm not surprised. Your host's cats ought to be exterminated!"

"I don't mean that. I suffer from insomnia."

"Ah. H'm. And what are the—er—symptoms?"

Eddy swallowed his annoyance at this display of inanity and said politely that the chief symptom was that he was usually awake when he wanted to be asleep.

"That's rather serious," said the doctor. "You probably suffer from anaemia—hence your nervousness, your hallucination and defective memory."

"I am hoping that you will prescribe some sleeping-pills."

"A very happy idea."

The doctor handed over the prescription, and Eddy paid his fee and departed.

On the way back to the house he went into a confectioner's and bought some cream cakes, knowing that the gluttonous girl was fond of sweets more than anything else. At the appropriate moment, after dinner, when no one else was in the room, he offered her the cakes. As usual, she pretended not to be interested in them and said she would take the rest up to her room and give them to her cats.

Eddy was certain that she would polish them all off while still walking up the stairs. Nor did he guess wrong. He had mixed into the cream some of the crushed sleeping-pills and within one hour, Grete was snoring so loudly that her cats ruffled their hair and arched their backs and huddled together in a corner of her bedroom.

•2•

It was a pitch-dark night with dirty weather blowing up.

The decisive hour had come, when he would suffer disappointments no longer. He took with him a roll of paper which he had smeared with pitch. His idea was to use his diamond ring to cut a square out of the window-pane in Grete's window then stick the soft tar-paper over the cut glass so as to lift it out noiselessly. Otherwise he would have had to push the glass in, making far too much disturbance. A long stout rope completed his equipment.

The weather could not have been more favourable for his undertaking. The deadly *Föhn* was blowing from the Alps, bringing with it heavy squalls of rain; thick clouds drew a pall of mourning above the countryside. Eddy climbed the winding staircase which led up to the projecting, ornamental tower room. This room had a sky-light, which opened easily, and through this it was quite simple to get out on to the roof.

Once there he felt like shouting a *Tally-ho* to the pursuing wind, so boldly adventurous was his mood.

With his hair tossed by the wind, a rope over his arm and the tarry paper in his hand, he looked like an insane cowboy galloping across the prairie with his lasso and a scroll of lyric poetry.

A strong iron hook projected from under the lead guttering above the girl's window. He had observed this hook from the garden. Immediately below it was a round dummy widow, and still further below, the girl' balcony.

It was a pleasant thought for the prospective burglar that his victim was locked in drugged slumber.

He attached one end of the rope to the hook in a sailor's sling, and allowed the other end to swing to and fro in the wind; it hung far below the level of Grete's balcony. He then tucked the tarry paper under his arm and climbed down.

But he felt the strip of blackened paper beginning to wind itself round his arm and as he tried to remove it the wind pressed the whole thing to his face. He now looked like a member of the Ku-Klux-Klan. Luckily he had reached the dummy window and could therefore perch himself on the narrow window ledge. He let go of the rope for a moment so that he could pull the tarry paper from his face. Grete's balcony was still two floors below him.

Only a short distance away he could see the swaying boughs of a giant pine, and as he sat precariously on the narrow window ledge he wondered why anyone should have thought of building this folly of a dummy window. He was, however, rudely awakened from these musings by the sudden realization that the dangling rope had disappeared. The wind had caught it as it swung to and fro and it was now entangled in the branches of the pine.

True, it might become disentangled and come swinging back to him at any moment; still, what with being stranded on a narrow ledge with his back to the wall, four storeys up and with nothing but a roll of tarry paper to hold on to, Eddy realized that so long as his rope remained in the pine-tree he was himself, so to speak, up a gum-tree.

He had only to stretch out his arm to seize the rope, but in his position he dared not make any movement at all.

He began to feel giddy and thought he would surely tumble to the ground.

There was nothing for it—he would have to wait for the next gust of wind to swing the rope back to him. It was not a night when one had to wait long for gusts of wind. One of them was coming along already, wild and roaring.

The rope jerked, become airborne—and was lashed securely between two braces. Now nothing less than a tornado would set it swinging again.

•3•

Eddy's situation was desperate. Compared with this his lumber-room vigil ending in the early morning cross-country race plus a swim had been almost fun and games.

He screwed himself into a ball to wedge himself against the dummy-window. He was numb with cold, soaked to the skin and it was still hours till down.

And when morning came, as it inevitably would—what then? How would he explain his curious position?

The gravel crunched. Somebody was coming! A broad-rimmed hat appeared.

It was Herr Maxl! The poet who had written *Wilhelm Tell*! What was he doing here?

Eddy remembered seeing the man strolling beside the fence with Frau Victoria, Head Gardener Krüttikofer's wife the other night. Aha! So that was the explanation! The Head Gardener had been called away to Erlenbach and was no doubt spending the night there. There was hope for Eddy now. He cleared his throat and called down from his eyrie.

"Good evening, Herr Maxl."

The poet looked up. It took him a moment to locate the owner of the voice, then he raised his hat.

"Good evening, Mr. Rancing. Rotten weather we're having tonight."

"Comes from the Alps. Must be a thaw," Eddy shouted, smiling wanly in his niche.

"Would it be impertinent to ask what you're doing up there?"

"Well... er... I couldn't tell..."

"Ah, in that case I mustn't disturb you," Herr Maxl said, raising his hat, and moving away.

"Herr Maxl... er... I wonder, can you see your way to help me?"

"I regret very much, Mr. Rancing, but I haven't a bean. However, Herr Hüggeli, the manager of the savings bank..."

"I don't mean financially. I should like to get down from here."

"Aren't you all right up there?... What's your idea? Trying to add a bit of statuary to the stonework, or something?"

"I can't get down."

"That doesn't tell me why you're up there..."

"The wind has blown the rope away and it caught in that pine over there. You might help me to get down from here, Herr Maxl."

"That depends altogether on me. I am willing to facilitate your descent, but first you absolutely must drop some trifling thing for me. For instance, you have a very fine watch and chain."

Eddy was shocked.

"This is blackmail!"

"You can leave that to my conscience. Well? Will you or won't you?"

Herr Maxl had always rather fancied Mr. Rancing's watch with its thick, short chain. He wasn't at all sure, however, that it was real gold. Once, in Zürich, he had bought a silver-headed cane and later he found that it was made of tin. He was more suspicious these days. He made as if to go.

"Wait!"

With silent contempt, Eddy flung his pocket-watch to the ground where it fell with a muffled thud in a flower-bed, among seedlings wrapped in paper.

"For shame!" he cried. "Fancy a poet being so materialistically minded!"

"There you're wrong. As a poet I'm not materialistically minded at all. I've never been paid a penny yet for my works. Now where is that bally watch?"

For now he couldn't find the thing. The wind howled, it was pouring with rain and Eddy was sure he'd catch pneumonia. At last the watch was found.

"Now get me down from here," Eddy urged.

"Look. I have been deceived once before. So if you don't mind, I will just go off to have it valued before we do anything."

Eddy very nearly fell headlong from his perch at that.

"But I say! Dash it, I may fall down any minute!"

"You must shut your eyes and pray. I'll just step round to Högraben's: he lives less than fifteen minutes from here. Excellent watchmaker. One of the best. Learned the trade at Schaffhausen. His younger sister is married to a painter. I'll ask him to take a look at this watch, and if he says it's gold, I'll come straight back to help you."

"Herr Maxl! You're a..."

"Don't thank me. I'll be as quick as I can. He gives twice who gives quickly."

Eddy wished he could give the poet something twice and give it quickly, but at last the poet set out.

Eddy had to cling on with all his might, resisting the force of the wind which now began to drive frozen sleet into his face, and his clothes looked like candied peel.

Herr Högraben's shop must have been a long way away or he must have been fast asleep; for it was quite forty-five minutes before the poet returned.

"It's all right," Herr Maxl reassured Eddy. "He says it's real gold. Now you'll be all right soon. Have no fear."

"A ladder... Get me a ladder," Eddy gasped.

"Don't need it. The fire-brigade will bring their own."

A siren sounded in the distance.

"You skunk! Have you gone and called out the fire-men?"

"Why, the gas company can't get you down."

"You'll find a ladder over there... I beseech you... Be-fore they arrive..."

"Oh, yes. And get myself fined for raising a false alarm. No fear, I say, how many jewels are there in this watch?"

·4·

Meantime the fire-brigade had turned out, headed by Unteroffizier Zobelmann. The fire-engine, complete with pump and ladder, came along with all the furious speed of the 3.5 h. p. provided by three horses and a mule.

Zobelmann's first action on receiving the call had been to sound the siren so as to give the people time to get to the scene of the disaster while the firemen were still making their preparations. Quickly he changed into his blue-and-white gala uniform. He would have to put his best foot for-ward today! This was a rare occasion! They hardly ever had a decent fire in this foul hole of a village.

"Ready? Then let her go!"

And the fire-engine raced along to the sound of horses' hooves and a ringing bugle.

By this time a large crowd had collected outside Wollishof Hall. Curious eyes were directed towards the pitiful figure sitting in the dummy-window, his trousers, like secondary water-pipes, spouting rain.

Now, with a great clatter, the fire-engine rolled to a halt. There followed some brief manoeuvering with the ladder. First they shoved it forward, then they shoved it back. At last, one of the men climbed up and lashed his right hand and leg to the topmost rung. He held up his other hand to the crowd; as a stunt, it was phenomenal and the chap got a big hand.

"Up we go!" Zobelmann bellowed.

Presently the ladder knocked against the wall, and Herr Lübli, the foreman, began to ascend.

By now the gaping crowd had swollen to comprise the total population of Mügli am See; every man, woman and child was present.

It was the merest chance that the firemen were not beaten to the start in the rescue operations by Herr Wollishoff. The old gentleman had been sleeping the sleep of the just when his daughter woke him up at about one o'clock in the morning. Grete had been awakened by an attack of nausea, otherwise known as the tummy rumbles, as a result of the large dose of sodium bicarbonate the doctor had prescribed for Eddy. Doctor Rüdiger had had second thoughts about his diagnosis and had persuaded himself that Eddy's insomnia was imaginary, and that he was really suffering from anaemia; he had therefore rung up the chemist and told him to hand out sodium bicarbonate on the prescription for veronal. And so Grete had awakened, seen the crowds and heard the arrival of the fire-brigade; alarmed, she had rushed to awaken her father.

Herr Wollishof tumbled into his dressing-gown and rushed out into the garden. He watched the men manoeuvering their ladders, saw their objective and rushed back into the house; when he came out again he was clutching an air-gun, which he proceeded to aim at the human bird perched above Grete's balcony.

He would have saved everyone a lot of trouble, to be sure, had he actually picked off his guest from the ledge of the dummy-window; and Eddy himself was past caring by now. However, at the last moment, Zobelmann halted the old man with a gesture.

"You should put something on!" he bellowed into Herr Wollishof's ear. "You may catch a cold!"

"I'll shoot the feller!"

"Not before we've got him down! What do you think we've turned out for? Now, two men restrain Herr Wollishoff!" he commanded.

The rescue operations were resumed and less than half an hour later, amid much cheering and waving of hats, the strange foreigner touched down. In hoarse, screeching tones not unlike the wailing of a siren, Eddy explained to the old man, who was still pinioned by two of the rescue team, that he was desperately in love with his daughter and had been meaning to propose to her.

"I meant to confess my love to her in a romantic balcony scene."

"What scene?" Herr Wollishoff roared.

"Young lover turns up at night under balcony to confess his love! It's a nice way of saying it! Been written by a great poet!"

"It was me," Herr Maxl muttered. "It happens to Wilhelm Tell."

"I love your daughter," Eddy screeched. "Want to marry her."

"What does he say?" the host asked Foreman Lübli, who stood next to him, hose in hand.

"He loves your daughter," bellowed Lübli in a voice that rattled the window-panes like a medium force gale.

"He loves your daughter!" roared the crowd with one voice.

"Water?... Water?... stammered the old man, astounded, and turned to stare in the direction of the lake.

But Grete, who had been standing in the background, moved forward and threw herself on Eddy's chest. Now, at last the old man had no difficulty in understanding the situation, and he turned and went indoors again.

In the morning light, the peaks of the Alps emerged from a sea of clouds that looked like tufts of wool and puffs of steam.

Later that morning, Eddy Rancing sent a telegram to his uncle:

Engaged to Buddha. Come immediately.

Eddy

CHAPTER SEVEN. *Lord Bannister creates a sensation in a freshly laundered dressing-gown. He survives the loss of his dress suit. Evelyn gives a brilliant performance at the wheel of an Alfa-Romeo. They meet three cows. His lordship relaxes somewhat but his agitation returns when he discovers the loss of his toilet case. Reappearance of the three cows. Lord Bannister and Evelyn don folk costumes in Lyons, take leave of each other, then continue their journey together. Newspaper headlines have a disastrous effect on Lord Bannister.*

·1·

They drove past a number of small villages. Lord Bannister forgot to worry about his dress clothes except when his flesh was pierced by a stud whenever he leaned forward.

Evelyn broke the silence.

"Ha-have you any idea," she said timidly, "where we can find the nearest garage where I could hire a car?"

For a few seconds, he wondered if he should answer her question at all. At last he decided that it was his duty to give at least a curt reply.

"There is one, so far as I know, at La Roselle. It's quite a big place. I hope I'll also find some appropriate accommodation there till tomorrow."

Again they relapsed into silence.

Trees painted with white bands were racing past them like an army of legless soldiers. The ancient beauty of the countryside had been spoiled by this ungainly belt of whitewash for the sake of motorists.

Lord Bannister continued to mutter to himself, since the thought of accommodation now reminded him of the possibility of another calamity he had luckily avoided.

"It's a mercy I always keep my toilet case in the car," he mumbled.

The small patent leather case lay on the seat beside him.

"Why a mercy?" inquired Evelyn, somewhat nervously.

"Otherwise I shouldn't be able to shave at La Roselle tomorrow morning. And I hate going about with a stubby chin."

"What a prig!" she thought; and when she inspected her own condition—bruised and scratched all over, her clothes torn and spattered with mud, chased by thugs in the middle of the Continent—she very nearly burst into tears. And this stuffed shirt was worried about his shaving-kit!

But perhaps her anxious effort to scorn Lord Bannister sprang from an involuntary desire to allay the suspicion that she was developing a more tender regard for the man.

She was still clutching her handbag, also of black leather, conscious that it contained the important orange-coloured envelope which was to pay for the Dreaming Buddha!

And also that unfortunate Commander Brandon's honour. What was the alias under which he was serving in the legion?

Münster... Münster... Münster...

She repeated the name as if to memorise a lesson.

At last, they reached La Roselle.

Lord Bannister pulled up outside the only inn in the village, and when he emerged in all the splendour of white tie-and-tails he caused quite a sensation among locals who happened to be snipping their wine there. Lord Bannister blushed to the roots of his hair when a short, red-headed, bandy-legged fellow walked all round him, eyeing him up and down as if he was a dashed advertisement kiosk. One vine dresser suggested in an audible whisper to the innkeeper that perhaps they'd better send for the district health officer while some of the boys were about.

Lord Bannister's trousers were patterned with oil stains. His shirt-collar, drenched and screwed up like a concertina, had chafed his neck and the crouched, driving position in which he had been sitting had caused his collar-stud to leave a deep imprint on his throat.

"Could you direct me to a garage, please?" Evelyn asked the *patron*.

"You'll find one next-door, *madame*. Some ten yards from this place. This way. You'll see a large barrel outside the entrance."

"Thank you... Could you please have a parcel of cold meat and fruit made up for me? I'll come back for it when I have hired a car."

"Very good, *madame*."

"I would like to book a room," Lord Bannister said.

The night patrol peered through the window of the bar and crossed himself.

"I can give you a quiet room on the first floor overlooking the garden," the innkeeper said. "Er," he added, somewhat hesitantly, "have you no attendant with you, sir?"

"I've had to drive the lady here urgently. Hadn't time to change... Will you please tell these people here to stop gaping at me. Or at least to stop feeling me."

As he snorted fiercely after the last word, the peasants scampered away from him in alarm, and listened uneasily to the vine-dresser's account of how the double-bass player of the Corbeille players' company had gone mad and walked about the village at night, wearing a silver crown on his head and pretending to be a widowed queen.

"Will you be taking a dinner?"

"No! I want to sleep!" He said firmly as if everyone was opposed to the idea.

Now at last Evelyn ventured to hold out her hand on him.

"God bless you for what you've done for me."

"That's all right."

They shook hands briefly.

Long after the door had shut behind her he continued to gaze after the girl. How sadly, how hesitantly she had walked away!

He swallowed, trying to reject the feeling of bitterness with which their encounter had left him. He felt sorry for the girl.

At least that is how he accounted for the vague uneasiness which made him want to say a few soothing words to her and to go with her part of the way.

He went up to his room. The innkeeper offered him one of his freshly laundered dressing-gowns.

After the exhausting journey, Lord Bannister ached in every limb. He found that he had left his toilet case in the car but was too weary to fetch it; he need not shave until morning. For the moment, his only concern was to go to bed. To bed! To bed! The innkeeper's freshly laundered dressing gown had a musty smell, but he could scarcely care about that; he wanted only to sleep... to sleep.

This vexatious adventure had quite exhausted him. He had found all that excitement very trying; he loathed unclear, awkward and embarrassing situations.

He flung himself down full length on the bed and stretched his limbs contentedly.

He switched the light off, happy in the knowledge that the incident was safely in the past, and before long he was sleeping soundly and deeply.

But he had slept soundly and deeply for only ten minutes when he was shaken out of his sleep.

Evelyn was standing by his bed, whispering into his ear: "Hurry! You must climb through the window immediately! I've propped a ladder against the window-sill."

·2·

Evelyn had arranged to hire a car from the owner of the garage, and then hurried back to the inn. She was only a few yards away when there was a flash of headlights and the sound of a car braking to a sudden halt. Six men jumped out of the car, and she had just time to conceal herself behind a nearby tree to avoid being seen. She immediately recognised Adams and Gordon; that gaudily dressed, monocled man with them too. Evidently the men had been in hot pursuit all the way from Paris but their car had been outstripped. They held a brief discussion. Concealed behind her tree, Evelyn could hear every word.

"It seems they've been fools enough to put up at this inn," said Adams. "We got to dispatch 'em. Both of 'em."

"Wait a minute," Gordon said, after peering through the window. "There are three blokes in there. Better wait till they've gone. Our two little birds can't get away from here anyway. So we might as well go in quietly and sit down. We've got them in our hands."

Meanwhile it had begun to rain. The six sinister-looking men went into the bar. Evelyn had stopped trembling; custom can make one calm even before the threat of death. She was now more alarmed by the news that these thugs proposed to kill that splendid personality, the kind-hearted Lord Bannister, the man for whom, in spite of his moroseness, she had come to feel such a warm regard. She peered through the window of the bar. The men were sitting in one corner, watching the door. Quickly, she walked back to the huge red car in which her pursuers had arrived.

She knew something about cars. When her father had been alive they had owned a large Ford which Evelyn had sometimes driven. Now her experience stood her in good stead. She screwed off the caps from all four tyres and loosened the valves until the air came rushing out. She opened the bonnet, snapped the cable leading to the magneto and allowed the water and oil to escape. Then she hurried to the rear of the building. As there was only one room overlooking the garden, she could not go wrong. Lord Bannister was sleeping behind the open window of the first-floor room. Luckily, she found a ladder leaning against the door of the loft; she had to use all her strength to manoeuvre this to the window-sill, then, with trembling knees, she began to climb. It was the first time she had ever climbed a ladder.

•3•

Lord Bannister sat up in bed; an oath rose to his lips, but when he looked at the girl, the words stuck in his throat.

"For heaven's sake... I beseech you!" she said. "Please don't ask any questions. Come with me at once or you'll be killed. There is a gang of murderers down in the bar. They may come here any moment! Please, please, don't lose a second! They think you're in it too. I overheard them say that they'd shoot you!"

A cold shiver ran down Lord Bannister's spine. He knew that she was speaking the truth. He slipped into his shoes.

"No! Don't dress! A single moment may cost us our lives. You can buy clothes anywhere on the way. Come on! Please!"

Lord Bannister picked up his wallet, wrapped a towel round his neck, then, wearing only his patent-leather shoes and the innkeeper's freshly laundered dressing-gown, followed the girl down the ladder. It was pouring with rain.

They reached the Alfa-Romeo in safety. Seconds went by before the engine began to purr, seconds seemed hours.

Then they were away.

On the instant, warned by the roar of the accelerating engine, the gangsters came tumbling out of the inn.

But the car was already racing towards the main road, raising fountains of mud on either side. The gangsters could pursue them only with bullets, one of which went straight through the rear window and through the windscreen between Evelyn and Lord Bannister. Both heard the brief, swift whizz past their ears; and Lord Bannister was compelled to admit later that in describing their situation Evelyn's account of their perilous plight was no more than sober truth.

They were putting distance between them and dangerous La Roselle at 70 m.p.h. and it was a happy thought for Evelyn that the gangsters must be stamping their feet in impotent rage around their unroadworthy car. Of course they might try hire the village grocer's Mercedes-Benz, but it was a museum piece and its chances of overtaking their Alfa-Romeo were about equal to those of a cow attempting to chase a golden eagle.

Frankly, the appearance of Lord Bannister, clad in a sodden dressing-gown, with a towel around his tousled hair, was a sight rarely seen on the road to Lyons at night. At this moment, he would have been happy to put on even his tails.

Evelyn's dress, too, was soiled, crumpled and torn.

"Don't you think, Miss Weston, that you're going a bit far in honouring me with your confidence by calling in my aid to this extent?" he said in a whisper, for his throat felt strained and sore. "Furthermore, if it isn't impertinent to ask: What is the cause for which you are risking my life?"

"I'm carrying a man's honour in my handbag."

"Is it possible that the family jewel has undergone such a metamorphosis? On the channel boat, when you first upset my night's repose—I do not say this to reproach you, for I have become accustomed to these invasions—you said you wanted me to help you to recover some family jewel. Yet now I find myself, in my dressing-gown, tearing along at 70 m.p.h. like a madman, making for Lyons, to save the honour of a gentleman I do not know. I hope I am not a coward, Miss Weston, but I consider I am acting within my rights if I object to your attempt to foist upon me the combined duties of a film star and an officer of the fire-brigade. To say nothing of being obliged to risk my paltry life..."

Without warning, Evelyn threw herself on his shoulder and again broke into bitter sobs. Lord Bannister muttered a smothered imprecation, then subsided into silence. Through villages and townships they sped without once slackening speed. He was resolved not to slow down until he found a shop at which he could buy himself a suit. Day was beginning to break.

"There are many things about which I must not speak," Evelyn sobbed. "But, believe me, I am an honest girl. I apologise for exposing you to so much danger, but I couldn't help it."

"I wish I could at least have a shave," he muttered. His untidy state gave him an almost physical pain. He felt somewhat embarrassed, too, for she had stopped crying and there was no longer any reason why she should rest her head on his shoulder. 'It would be quiet ridiculous,' he found himself thinking, 'if I were to kiss her after what I've just said.' He couldn't imagine how he had come to harbour such an extraordinary idea.

For her part, Evelyn was hoping that her seemingly absentminded posture would not strike him as peculiar; she found it most agreeable. She was so grateful for the agreeable sensation that she relaxed and closed her eyes; the next minute she was actually sleeping on Lord Bannister's shoulder. Every now and then as they raced along, he would steal a sideways glance at her, and mutter incomprehensibly.

'She's most peculiar,' he though; 'I've only seen her in three conditions so far: running away, crying, and sleeping.'

·4·

In the bleak light of day, the situation became decidedly awkward. The occupants of oncoming cars nearly ditched their vehicles in surprise as they saw at the wheel of the approaching Alfa-Romeo a man who looked like a mad athlete, supporting on his shoulder some poor beggar-woman. As the traffic increased they attracted more and more attention. He thought with exasperation of the scandal that was bound to ensue once he was recognised as the English nobleman whose scientific lecture had been prominently reported in the morning papers.

"Look," said Evelyn, who had been thinking along similar lines; "I know how to drive a car. Suppose you let me take the wheel?"

"And what about me?" he said suspiciously.

"Well... You might... perhaps... get behind the front seat... and huddle up on the floor... You'd escape detection that way..."

"Do you insist on this new stunt? I can't tell you how deplorably the instruction of acrobatics is neglected in the medical faculties of universities. Still, if you insist—I give in."

"Oh dear. Why do you scoff at me? I am concerned for your reputation."

"I too have an idea that this is not how my admirers imagine me to look... Oh no! Don't do that. I can't stand the sight of tears... Very well, I'll go and double myself in two and tie myself in a knot. I only hope I won't have to do a trapeze stunt."

He relinquished his seat at the wheel, clambered into the back of the car and, groaning miserably, crouched on the floor, hugging his knees. In the meantime, they had stopped to fill up with petrol.

From now on, she would be in charge. Unfortunately the youth at the filling-station noticed an elderly lady with short hair was hiding on the floor of the car, and he called out his mother and sister, three younger brothers and a grandfather. The clan gathered round the car and stared at Lord Bannister through the windows as if he was a shark in a fish-tank. One of the children ran off the village to tell his friends. As soon as the tank was full, they drove quickly on.

Lord Bannister had ceased his reproaches. He said nothing. He sat on the floor, hugging his knees and contemplating his muddy ankles which showed above his patent-leather shoes, and smoked listlessly like one who despairs of any improvement in his lot.

Later, like some tamed beast of prey, he endured his captivity with melancholy stoicism while Evelyn brought tea and sandwiches from a pub, fed them to him, waited patiently till he finished his tea, and returned the dishes. During this repast, the village priest happened to pass by; he stopped by the car, peered inside and suggested that Evelyn should hire a strong peasant lad from the village to accompany her for the rest of the journey so that she would have someone to help her to attend to the patient. Lord Bannister was shocked to hear her thank the priest for his advice and declare that she needed no assistance, since her unfortunate brother was behaving calmly.

In describing his behaviour as calm, Evelyn was speaking the truth. Lord Bannister *was* behaving calmly for a man who had achieved remarkable results in cutting sleeping-sickness and was a hopeful candidate for this year's Nobel Prize. For a man of his reputation and standing, and considering that he was constrained to sit cowering on the floor of his car, rigged out in a freshly laundered dressing-gown belonging to the innkeeper of La Roselle, with a towel wrapped round his neck, his hair dishevelled and his legs spattered with mud, it was no exaggeration to say that Lord Bannister was behaving calmly.

And as it was the Blonde Hurricane who was now at the steering-wheel, the Alfa-Romeo began to reveal that she was not unaffected by the change.

The front mudguards became dented, and the fender was twisted slightly in a minor brush with a level-crossing gate. Soon afterwards, the near-side door accidentally swung open as they were passing under a viaduct, and as she applied the brakes, a projecting buttress on the wall buckled the door so much that it was left looking like a concertina. This operation was accompanied by ear-splitting sounds of strained brakes and collapsing metal.

"I've still got to get my hand in," she said apologetically, over her shoulder.

"Oh, you have, have you, "Lord Bannister responded ruefully, removing some splinters of glass from his hair. At this moment, the car received a frightful jolt from the rear, and an eloquent Gallic oath issued from the car behind them. Evelyn drove on.

"Could you remember to draw in the indicator?" he pleaded. "You always leave it sticking out and the people behind think you are turning right; that's why they try to overtake you on the left, and one of them will certainly crash into us. The best idea is to retract the indicator immediately after use."

"But it won't retract!" she cried, turning a switch in despair.

"Not if you turn the switch for the wind-screen wipers. It's the one next to that. No! No! That's the tail lamp!... Oh... At last."

She stifled a sob.

"Don't," he said in a hoarse whisper, gently imploring, "No crying, please. I can't bear that sort of thing. Much rather have you sleeping or running away. No crying.

I don't even mind if, in the end, there are only three of us left: you, the steering-wheel and me... Ugh!... It's nothing. Only my head... May I ask you to be more careful when you change gear... Don't cry. You'll get your hand in. Oh, can you give me the iodine?"

In her anxiety to be able to give him the iodine promptly, Evelyn applied the hand-brake so vigorously that Lord Bannister was jerked against the door like a battering ram. He thought his head must be split open and to complete the illusion, there was at that precise moment a loud bang as the left rear tyre exploded. The vehicle shuddered, lurched and skidded, fortunately at a diminishing speed, towards a tree, where it came to rest, the radiator quite staved in, a melancholy sight indeed.

•5•

They set about changing the wheel.

While they were thus employed, a little boy came by leading three cows, and all four watched, wide-eyed with amazement, as the insane gentleman-driver crawled about in the dust under the vehicle. It seemed that Evelyn had still not got her hand in properly, for she had unfortunately dislodged the jack, and the car had fallen with such a thud that the dilapidated door had broken off and was now lying on the middle of the road; the jack was submerged beneath the chassis, and Lord Bannister had no alternative but to creep between the wheels to try and extricate it.

That was how matters stood at 11 a.m.

By 12.30, it seemed that the car might possibly be roadworthy again.

"Off we go!" said Evelyn.

"Let her rip!" exclaimed Lord Bannister and he resumed his position on the floor. With the assistance of the young cowherd, they had wedged the door behind the driving seat, and it was not fixed to anything, it fell, from time to time, on Lord Bannister's head; but such trifles were as nothing to him now.

Evelyn prepared to back the car away from the battered tree-trunk and the young cowherd made a hasty retreat with his cows to watch from safe distance. The engine emitted a singing whine like the last notes of a dying tenor and stopped immediately. Evelyn tried again. This time she managed to put the engine into gear, and she accelerated: the engine roared for a second and then stopped again. Lord Bannister peered above the door he was now holding in his arms.

"Try reverse," he suggested. "We haven't a ghost of a chance of felling that big tree and going over it, you know!"

Poor Evelyn realised that she had engaged in bottom gear; now, after a few unsuccessful attempts, she managed to adjust the gear lever.

Slowly the car slid back from the tree. Something fell to the ground with a clatter—the bumper this time. They made place for it next to the door; Lord Bannister was by now travelling in the company of a number of spare parts.

However, in spite of these minor losses, they found they were able to race along at a good speed.

"You asked for the iodine," she said.

Lord Bannister, anticipating another application of the brakes, sought desperately to secure his position.

"Do you think I should risk it?"

"Here. Take your toilet case." She handed over the small leather case.

He opened it, but all he could see in it was an enormous orange-coloured envelope.

"Sorry, that's mine," she stammered, and quickly shut the case.

"First of all I want to have a shave; the iodine can wait," he declared resolutely.

She was exasperated.

"We are being followed! Think! If they haven't got a good car..."

"Miss Weston! On several occasions, you have managed to win me over to your somewhat peculiar views. This time you have absolutely no hope of doing so. No arguments, please. It's possible that we're being followed. It is also possible that we shall be killed. All the same, I intend to have a shave—and that's final! After that, let me fall if fall I must: I'll be a victim in the name of hygiene."

There was a touch of malicious pleasure in her voice as she now exclaimed, "Why, we've lost your toilet case somewhere!"

For the first time during the trip, he showed genuine alarm.

"Look carefully! It's impossible! My soap! My gargle! My shaving kit!"

"Oh!" At the moment she felt like killing him. Thinking of his shaving set and gargle at a time like this! What a cissie! This was a matter of life and death, he felt worried about the loss of his shaving kit!

"We must turn back at once!"

"But..."

"Miss Weston! You're wasting your breath."

"We would be driving into the jaws of deadly peril!

"Our trip hasn't been child's play so far. We have only survived because Providence is guiding our car in spite of our own activities. That should be a source of hope for us. Miss Weston! We must now turn back and find my toilet case!"

She saw that it would be useless to protest further.

In that moment, she conceived a violent hatred for that toilet case. She hated it fiercely and whole-heartedly, because she loved its owner, and the toilet case was in danger of spoiling their relationship.

Thus she ruminated as she turned the car about. First she went into reverse again so as to adjust the steering-wheel, and she backed straight into a tree. She turned round to see the cause of their sudden halt, inadvertently put her foot on the accelerator and shot the car into a lamp-pot. Lord Bannister said nothing. Supporting his chin in his cupped palms, he crouched sadly on the floor of his car, the very image of Marius meditating on the ruins of Carthage.

But the car, it seemed, was indestructible, and at last they started back along the road. Luckily, only a couple of miles back, they came upon the cowherd and his three cows once again, and saw that the boy was holding Lord Bannister's case. A few coins changed hands and the case was restored to its owner. It was an even luckier day for the boy who had also found a brand-new motor horn on the road, but he had not cared to mention this to this down-at-the-heel gentleman-driver.

"Let's hurry now!" she said agitatedly, pulling the first lever that came to hand, and causing yet another warning groan to issue from the engine. She drowned the noise with a blast on the klaxon, switched on the lights once or twice and, for no known reason, the sinister noise was silenced. By this time Lord Bannister had come to respect her quite individual style at the wheel. She always put her hand on the wrong switch, and yet the car was running.

"We will stop here," he said firmly. "I will now have a shave and comb my hair. Will you please pass me my toilet case."

"Here you are!" She flung the case back over her shoulder with such vehemence that it struck hard against the lamp lying on the back seat.

Angrily, she turned her back. Lord Bannister was a tidy soul, and he now placed the mudguard carefully on the seat so as to have some support for his mirror and shaving-dish, and then he started to shave.

While Lord Bannister was busy with his toilet, Evelyn walked impatiently up and down a little way off, on the highway.

Yet she would have done well to have shown more interest in Lord Bannister's mania of cleanliness.

Had she done so she would have seen Lord Bannister take from his toilet case a small enamelled box on the top of which there was a little ceramic statuette with bowed head representing the Buddha, and she would have seen that in this box the noble lord kept his shaving kit.

Yes, Lord Bannister kept his shaving kit in the box surmounted with the Dreaming Buddha, and he had not the faintest idea that he owned the world's most valuable toilet box, worth one million pounds sterling.

·6·

It was drizzling quietly and they travelled on the regular swishing sound of the windscreen wipers. There was nothing on the road except a few barrows laden with fruit and firewood coming from the opposite direction.

As they neared Lyons the oncoming traffic became heavier and Evelyn sounded her klaxon continuously to forge a way ahead for her zigzagging vehicle. Sometimes, by the way of more urgent signal, she would use in turn the klaxon, the sliding ash-tray, and the tail-lamp switch. Miraculously they met with no greater disaster than to overturn a barrow piled high with firewood, but they calmed the owner with a few francs. During the rest of the trip, the car consumed three chickens, one sheep-dog and two bicycles.

"There is less and less of this car," he remarked despondently. Doggedly she drove on.

Now they were in Lyons and she began to look forward to the prospect of buying a new dress and having a wash. There was so much traffic, she had to sound the klaxon every second. She would not have to do that in the centre of the city for fear of attracting attention. Suddenly she realised that the water in the radiator was boiling.

There followed an excruciating ten minutes in the middle of a crowd of onlookers. When they were able to go on again they found that hey had left the radiator cap on the pavement. But they could not worry about that, so great was their relief that they had arrived safely in Lyons. They were not likely to run into any serious trouble now, they thought.

They were wrong.

They slowed down, looking for a dress shop at which they could make an unobtrusive halt. But next time she sounded the klaxon she could not release the knob, and as she jabbed desperately at every button in sight, they lurched forward to the continuous piercing screech of the klaxon. Lord Bannister leaned over to give what assistance he could with his one available hand, for the other was wedged fast behind the mudguard. They were then overtaken by a lorry which brushed past them with only inches to spare and Evelyn, relaxing with relief, next overturned a barrow of fruit into the gutter.

So they made their noisy entry into Lyons, advertising their arrival like an emergency ambulance. Terrified citizens looked out of their windows; pedestrians stopped to stare and one butcher said knowingly to his customers:

"There has been a fire every day lately."

Evelyn let go of the steering-wheel with both hands and clapped her hands over her ears.

"Cut the wire!" Lord Bannister cried in exasperation.

She snipped widely: immediately the wind-screen wipers ceased to function.

"Stop! No more!" he entreated quickly.

He leaned forward and cut through the lead himself. It was fortunate that they were in a quiet side-street while engaged in these desperate activities for Evelyn in her excitement ran the car onto the pavement and had to make a detour round a telegraph-pole before getting back into the road.

"Of course," she panted triumphantly," when I do something well, as I did just now, you don't bother to praise me."

At last she spotted the long-desired dress shop.

"I can't go and buy you a suit until I have found something to wear myself," she said. "So don't think I am being selfish."

"You are a skilful and selfless person," he replied dryly. He was nervous because so many people stopped to gape at his car. Yet it was certainly worth a second glance. It looked like one of the old tractors one used to see with small travelling circus companies but now discarded for scrap; it was nothing more than a collection of parts hardly holding together. When Evelyn crashed the hand-brake to bring this pitiful wreck to a halt in front of the shop there was a clatter like that of a falling box full of pebbles.

She went into the shop and quickly made her purchases so that she would be presentable enough to shop for Lord Bannister. She even washed her face and hands in the shop, claiming that she had an accident. When she reappeared she was wearing an off-the-peg suit in which she looked like the wife of an assistant concierge dressed for a Sunday afternoon family visit.

When she came out of the shop, she had to push her way through the crowd which had collected round the car.

Evelyn then plunged into an arcade where she selected various items of clothing for Lord Bannister without too much regard for sartorial effect. Then she drove round and round the city while the noble lord performed the most agile feat he had attempted, for he managed to clothe himself in his new wardrobe while crouched in the back seat of the wrecked car. He was not unduly perturbed to find that she had chosen a Tyrolese hat with an outsize feather. A more painful choice was the checked plus-fours which should rather have been called minus, and a sea-green velvet jacket which flapped round his knees. In such garments he could hardly expect not to attract a crowd but he could at least travel in the normal way by sharing the front seat with the girl. When they drew up outside a hotel, the porter knew at a glance that he was opening the door for an eccentric corn-chandler and his wife who came from across the border.

"Lord Bannister," she murmured as soon as they were standing in the lobby, "the time has come when I need inconvenience you no longer."

"Miss Weston, from now on you should never say that. We are all in God's hands, more or less. I would only ask you this: when you next need me, don't wait till I have gone to sleep. In return, I promise you that from this day on I'll do some exercises every day." Once again he saw her eyes fill with tears. "Don't you think you had better be frank with me and make a clean breast of it? You may yet need the assistance of a man."

"I can't. I should only drag you into danger. I am very grateful for what you have done for me. In this case I am carrying the honour of a very unhappy gentleman; an honour with which my own happiness is not unconnected. I have inherited a vast fortune, but I must find it for myself and I am now on the right trail. I must go to Morocco. That is all I can disclose. You have every right to curse the day you ran into me."

"I think that's something of an exaggeration, don't you know. You might say that now and then while in your company, I have not always found the comfort and luxury to which I am accustomed but that's all. By the way, if you're bound for Morocco you might make a trip together with me tomorrow. I won't be going back to Paris now; I'll have my luggage sent after me."

"God forbid! You have exposed yourself to danger enough on my account, and I am happy to think that you've come through unscathed. Thank you... and goodbye."

He heard her ask the reception clerk at what time there was a flight for Morocco, and he heard the reply that a plane was due to take off in twenty-five minutes. Then she turned and left the hotel.

As on two previous occasions, Lord Bannister was left gazing after her with mixed feelings.

He seemed disturbed and unhappy whereas he should surely have felt relief at having rid himself of Evelyn Weston's inconvenient company.

What was this 'honour' she was talking about? No doubt, after all they had been through together, a more courageous man would continue to hover about this helpless and persecuted girl. She must think him a coward. He had been intent on saving his own skin, while Evelyn Weston continued her flight to Morocco.

She would go on running away, crying and sleeping.

She was at her sweetest when asleep, he decided.

He went up to his room looking forward to a nice long sleep himself.

He flung himself into an arm-chair, exhausted by the nightmarish car trips; then he rang for the porter and asked him to fetch his toilet case from the car. He was looking forward to a hot bath and was already imagining its soothing effect on every bone.

Through the window he could see his quondam car, from which the porter had no difficulty in extracting the toilet case: there wasn't even a door left for him to open.

The door, the mudguards, the bumpers and one reflector were stacked in the back seat and a crowd had gathered to wonder at the small heap of battered scrap iron which not so long before had been his elegant Alfa-Romeo.

The hot water gurgled into the bath and he was ready now for towel, soap, sponge. He opened the black case – and found in it a large orange-coloured envelope with five seals.

•7•

They had each taken the other's case, and Evelyn was on her way to Morocco carrying with her not the unknown gentleman's honour but Lord Bannister' razor and gargle!

Where now was his duty? This girl had risked death to gain possession of the envelope which he was now holding in his hand. There was no doubt as to his next step. He must follow her. He must go now, in the wake of the hurricane, all thought of his own comfort dismissed in the face of such devotion.

He saw his horror that it was already four o'clock and feared that he would miss the plane. It was all one with him now: he would arrange for his luggage to be sent on to Morocco when it arrived in Lyons from Paris.

And he would tell them to have the wreck of his car towed away and stored somewhere.

Ha cast a parting glance at the gurgling hot water... the turned down bed ... and was away.

He tipped the driver so generously that it could only be due to a watchful Providence that there were no fatal accidents on the road to the airport. As he leaped from the taxi he could see that the propeller was already revolving. There was just time for him to scramble through the door before the gangway was rolled away, and the plane began to move down the runway.

A cordial voice spoke by his side:

"Good afternoon, Lord Bannister. Lady Ann must have been worried that you were going to miss the plane. I say, where on earth did you get that marvellous hat?

It was editor Holler, who had left Paris by this very plane. It had taken him some seconds to recognise Lord Bannister under his Tyrolean folk costume; the learned gentleman appeared to have unconventional tastes in travelling costume.

•8•

When Evelyn noticed Lord Bannister, the sad expression on her face disappeared immediately and she glowed with hope and beauty.

"We have taken the wrong cases," he said as he lowered himself, panting, into the seat next to her. "I couldn't have kept with me the honour of an unknown gentleman."

Evelyn had not yet noticed the exchange. In dismay, she snatched at the case he handed to her, and heaved a sigh of relief when she saw that it still contained the envelope.

"I shall never be able to repay you for this," she breathed, handing over his toilet case which until then she had been jealously guarding.

"Be careful. You must call me Henry. That awful editor is on the plane and he's going to Morocco too. Look, he is coming now."

So he was. He was bringing coffee in a thermos-flask and several picnic cups.

"You must have come a formidable speed from Paris to have got to Lyons so soon," began Holler, as he poured out coffee.

"Yes. We had quite a good run."

They drank coffee.

"You look a bit tired, Lord Bannister," Holler said, eyeing that gentleman. "Yet I should imagine your car is pretty comfortable."

"Not always," said Lord Bannister ruefully. "What's the news in Paris?" he continued, trying to change the conversation from this painful subject.

"There's always something happening. You should always read the morning papers. The whole nation's in a ferment. Someone has quite by accident exposed a major espionage ring. True, their activities were directed against Britain, but as you know, that means that they were also opposed to France. Two killed, five seriously wounded, eighty arrests, and one hundred thousand francs reward for anyone giving information that could lead to the arrest of the ringleader. By the way, the master spy seems to be a compatriot of ours—a Miss Evelyn Weston. Hullo!... that went down the wrong way! Here, take this paper napkin."

Lord Bannister coughed helplessly and the obliging Holler sponged his lapel.

Evelyn sat as if frozen to her seat.

Lord Bannister had gone very pale, and he spoke in a hoarse whisper.

"How remarkable. Do you happen to have a morning paper with you?"

"Here you are."

Holler handed him the paper.

On the front page, in the boldest type ever used, Lord Bannister read the headline:

100,000 FRANCS REWARD FOR INFORMATION
LEADING TO THE ARREST OF EVELYN WESTON

There followed, in somewhat more modest type, a number of sensational sub-headings about police raids, assassinations, espionage, larceny and burglary; and all these activities were, without exception, closely associated with the name of the spy, Evelyn Weston. She was described as enemy Number One of both France and England, a woman who had stopped at nothing to possess herself of some vital military secret and who was Suspect Number One to the detectives who were looking for the murderer. The public were warned that she was armed and would be a dangerous adversary.

Next came two closely printed pages summarizing all the major crimes that had been committed in recent decades and commenting on them with reference to Evelyn Weston's possible complicity. The Paris police had for some months been observing the activities of a number of suspects. They had made no arrests, hoping to give the spies a false sense of security in which they might inadvertently reveal the whereabouts of a valuable document which had fallen into their hands. For some weeks past, a certain house had been under police observation. It would not have been in the public interest to disclose further details while the investigation was still in progress. The one item of information they now wished to make widely known was the name of the spy—Evelyn Weston. The entire district surrounding the key building was the headquarters of various international intelligence agents. The moment had come when it appeared that the man who had stolen the document wanted to sell it, and the police saw their chance to arrest a number of dangerous individuals. There was a large-scale police raid in which many persons were wounded. The raid had centred round the flat of a man who said to be a company manager and this flat had been virtually besieged by the police. Two individuals named Fleury and Donald were shot dead on the stairs. It was possible that here too the first shot had been fired by Evelyn Weston. The company manager was found mortally wounded inside the flat and some time later made a death-bed confession. It seemed that he had been shot by a fellow-spy with whom he had been bargaining.

Two other men escaped from the flat, one unidentified, the other a notorious intelligence agent, called Adams. The dying man had also revealed that a woman had been present in the apartment, and he had seen this woman snatch the precious document from the writing-desk, and run away with it. At that moment he had been hit by a bullet and could remember nothing more. He had, however, recognised the woman as the person who had visited him earlier that day to inquire about a ceramic statuette, when she had given her name as Evelyn Weston. It had been ascertained that Evelyn Weston had crossed the Channel on board the S.S.Kingsbay. A charwoman at the flat had given evidence that during the afternoon, Evelyn Weston had gained admittance to the apartment by posing as an employee from a delicatessen shop; it was possible that she had concealed herself in the apartment on that occasion.

Evelyn Weston was remarkably pretty, of medium height, blonde, etc.

CHAPTER EIGHT. *Lord Bannister believes that now he sees all. He does nothing of the sort. Lack of drains holds up a wedding. Arthur Rancing refunds even the fees of the assistant engineer. The national colours are hung out over the restaurant, but the community singers are very nearly not required. Eddy realises that his gamble has not come off, and waives his claim in his uncle's favour. Holler remains irrepressible. He takes the formidable fortress of Guéliz by storm; he goes shopping for Evelyn, and survives some hard bargaining; he knows of a link between an American symphony orchestra and the Sahara.*

·1·

Lord Bannister looked up. Now he understood all. But Holler was no longer beside him; he was suffering from air-sickness and had no wish to be seen in this condition by the lady. There were very few other passengers on board. An old couple were sitting in front; Holler's place was immediately behind them; then came several rows of unoccupied seats separating him from Lord Bannister and Evelyn. Thus nobody could possibly hear what they were saying.

"Can you forgive me?" Evelyn whispered.

"I cannot," said Lord Bannister.

"The facts given in the newspaper are correct but the interpretation is quite wrong. I am not a spy."

"Please don't bother to explain. You are very clever. And I have been very stupid. You have not behaved at all well towards me, and yet it pains me to be the one who will have to give you up to the police."

Her lips trembled.

"Do you mean to give me up to the police?"

"Did you think I would become your accomplice?"

"I haven't committed any crime. What is more, I am fighting to vindicate the honour of someone I have never seen. I don't care if you do give me up to the police. I should only be sorry to think that I would be the cause of your being arrested."

"Me arrested? What do you mean?"

"Of course, you would be able to clear yourself eventually. But you did bring me across the Channel, didn't you? You did make people believe I was your wife; and you did help me to escape from the scene of the crime. It will be very hard to convince the police that you didn't know what you were doing. Don't you agree, Lord Bannister?"

For a long while, he remained silent. Indeed, he had been with the girl from the start, and no one was likely to believe that they were chance companions. Even if he could get them to accept his own story, there would certainly be an awful scandal.

"Yes," he said at last. "You are right. I would be in a horribly tight corner. But I think it is more important to act honourably than to pander to public opinion. I have acted in good faith, even if my actions get me into trouble. It would be most dishonourable of me not to give you up to the police even if I did have to suffer for it myself."

There was a silence during which they watched the rain rushing past the windows.

"Well," she said, "*I* have got you into trouble, so let me make amends. There's no need to involve you at all. When we get to Marseilles, I will give myself up to the airport police under your very eyes. I'll give them the envelope and tell them that I am Evelyn Weston. Then I shall be arrested without your being involved at all."

"I agree to that. Let me warn you, however, that I'll be watching your every movement. You'd better not try any tricks with me. My honour will be in your hands."

"No one could be more concerned for your honour than me," she said in a muffled, quivering voice; and he gave her a surprised look. They were silent during the rest of the flight.

At Marseilles, all the passengers descended to stretch their legs and so no one found it peculiar to see Evelyn and Lord Bannister also taking a stroll. Suddenly she left his side and walked with resolute steps straight towards a door marked "Police." Lord Bannister followed her at a distance of some eight yards; then he was astounded to see her take from her handbag the large envelope with the five seals before quickening her pace.

What happened next Lord Bannister was ever afterwards at loss to explain, even to himself: it was if he had been pushed from behind: he hurried after her and caught her by the arm just as she reached the door.

"Wait," he said breathlessly. "I don't want you to... I don't care what you did... I couldn't bear you to be hurt... Put that envelope away!"

She obeyed him in alarm.

"Listen," he continued. "You are to fly on to Morocco and when you get there you may run away and do whatever you like. I don't want to know that you have been arrested. Do you understand? I'm sure I don't."

"B-but—why?"

"It may be stupid of me but I just don't want this to happen. That's all."

When the plane took off once again, they were sitting side by side in sorrowful silence.

Lord Bannister was deathly pale.

•2•

"You are both so kind that if you both wanted to marry me I wouldn't know which of you to choose," said Grete, with a seven-inch smile. It was then that Mr. Arthur Rancing conceived a deep respect for his nephew, who was planning to marry this female for the paltry sum of one million pounds. It was simply nothing for such a heroic deed.

Next, Arthur Rancing went to see old Wollishoff. He had brought from Zürich a present of a hearing aid for his host so they were able to talk in comfort. He would have gone mad otherwise.

"A Wollishoff girl must bring to her marriage a sum large enough to enable the couple to settle down on a respectable fashion," said the bride's father.

"That's just I expected to hear from you," replied A.B.C.D. (Arthur Bede Cecil David) Rancing. "That's the way to talk! Just what one would expect of a true Helvetian gentleman! You can't deny that you are an industrial consultant. In England, industrial consultants are held in great respect."

"I ask nothing in return, except that Mr. Rancing should love my daughter."

"Herr Wollishoff, I know my family. My nephew Edward adores your daughter. He is half-mad with love for her. Can't sleep at night."

"I know. The doctor's told me about that. He'll get over it though. He ought to take digestion tablets..."

"What, in your opinion, would be a suitable date for the wedding?"

Wollishoff reflected.

"Well, I think... Would Whitsun be all right?"

It was now three and a half weeks before Whitsun.

"Perfectly. Whitsun," Arthur Bede Rancing continued, waxing lyrical, "it's the day of flowers and loving hearts. Whitsun will be a most suitable date."

"That's what I think too. Well, then, the wedding can take place two years from Whitsun."

Seconds later Arthur Rancing had still forgotten to replace his jaw.

"It cannot take place sooner than that on any account," Wollishoff continued. "And even another six months after that wouldn't make much difference, I think."

"Do you really mean that? But it's impossible."

"Why should it be impossible? I have told you that my daughter cannot enter her marriage just anyhow. Unfortunately, some of the entries about certain technical aspects of the sewerage system were found to be incorrect last year. I had been put in charge of the drainage system for the town..."

"But there are no drains in this place at all!"

"That's the trouble, my dear Mr. Rancing. I had been given the task of providing them, and I have not succeeded. You see, drains cost money. See what I mean? We haven't got the drains yet, but we have had expenses. I couldn't tell you myself how it all happened. As my uncle happens to be an influential man, they have been content to confiscate my property pending reimbursement of the expenditure incurred in local development. And such developments cost a lot of money. You can take that from me. I happen to have had some experience. It'll take me at least two years to refund the sum, even if I hand over my total income for the purpose. I am not the first nor the last of those who sacrifice everything they possess to promote the development of their native country."

"You don't mean to say you want your daughter to wait all that time?"

"Why not? When she's already been waiting so long? She waited for her first fiancé for five years; but he volunteered and was taken prisoner."

"Yes, I know. A number of Swiss fought with the French..."

"This was with the Japanese. In the Russo-Japanese war. She had another fiancé who fought for the French."

"That's a fine tradition, to be sure. Still, two years is such a long time..."

"It's no use arguing, sir. A Wollishoff girl shall not marry while her father is threatened with criminal proceedings."

Neither argument for petition was of any avail; Herr Wollishoff remained obstinate in his decision.

The two Rancings paced up and down the guest-room in despair.

"A pretty kettle of fish, this!" A.B.C.D. Rancing raged. "Here we are, with a diamond worth one million pounds sterling housed under the same roof, and we can't do anything about it."

"How much did the deaf old bounder pinch, anyway?" said E.F.G.H. (Edward Frederic George Henry) Rancing.

"I took a cursory look at the books and from what I could see I gather there was a deficit of about two thousands pounds."

"Then don't be ridiculous, uncle! You have only to hold out your hand and there's one million quid for the taking; yet you're allowing a paltry sum like that to stand in your way! Come on, fork it out!"

A.B.C.D. stood still in perplexity.

"What are you thinking about?" E.F.G.H. continued vehemently. "We'll get five hundred thousand quid each, and so far it's been I who have done all the work. You've done nothing but wait for the plum to fall into your lap. The least you could do would be to put your hand in your pocket now and then. You won't? Very well, Good-bye."

Impetuously, he snatched up his hat. He was seriously resolved to quit. Recent events had told upon his nerves. He was emaciated, his pale face showed signs of latent neurosis; and ever since that balcony scene, he had been tormented by rheumatism. For him Mügli am See had been the scene of much suffering.

"Wait!" A.B.C.D. cried. "That's not such a bad idea of yours."

Three days later, to the utter astonishment of the authorities, Herr Wollishoff refunded the entire deficit which included the fees for a quite imaginary assistant-engineer.

•3•

For the inhabitants of Mügli am See, Whitsuntide dawned cool, fine and sunny. It was the wedding day of old Wollishoff's daughter and crowds of folk in their best clothes paraded the streets, anxious to see the sights. On three previous Sundays the banns had been read by the priest. The lattice garden gate was, for some unknown reason, pasted all over with coloured paper, and the valet and the porter were wearing new liveries given to them by Mr. Arthur B.C.D. Rancing. Victoria, Head Gardener Krüttikofer's wife, had been swept clean. The national colours had been hung above the local restaurant.

That was how matters stood at 10 a.m.

At that hour precisely, Eddy Rancing picked up the morning paper, which had been placed beside his plate. He then swallowed a large piece of a crusty roll and for a few seconds was unable to breathe at all for there on the front page, in the boldest type ever used, was the headline:

100,000 FRANCS REWARD FOR INFORMATION
LEADING TO THE ARREST OF EVELYN WESTON

His eyes flew over the print. What was this? Evelyn a spy? And what was she doing in France? For Eddy loved Evelyn and had been planning all along to marry her as soon as he had money to support her, and had even decided that if she refused his hand in marriage he would nevertheless give her a suitable share of the price of the diamond.

He turned over the pages of the newspaper and for the second time was afflicted with the same difficulty in breathing.

Lord and Lady Bannister, said the caption; but the picture showed Evelyn, wearing a kimono, standing at the door of a state-room on board ship in the company of an exceedingly startled looking gentleman. There was no doubt about it—it *was* Evelyn Weston! He used to see her in that kimono on the King's Road for a couple of seconds every morning when she took the milk from the doorstep.

But what was the explanation of the photographs? On the front page she was wanted by the police; and on the back page she was the wife of the celebrated scientist! Eddy's head swam with confused thoughts.

Below the picture, there was a brief account of the tremendous interest aroused by the lecture Lord Bannister gave in Paris. Lady Bannister had accompanied her husband to Paris but she had been indisposed and unable to attend the lecture. Naturally she had not been present at the lecture; what she had been doing, it seemed, was to break into a house, steal some important document and get away. Leaving a couple of corpses in her wake.

Eddy was worried. For the first time, his instinct told him that something had gone badly wrong. What was the clue that had brought her to France? For that she was there to look for the Buddha, Eddy had no doubt whatever.

Uneasily, he took the ales ledger from his trunk. But there was no mistaking the entry. One single "Dreaming Buddha" had been sold in May, along with the "Harvesters", and both pieces had been sent here, to Herr Wollishoff.

Then why had she gone to Paris? And, according to the newspaper, she had been enquiring after some ceramic statuette…

He sat still, brooding, and as he did so his glance fell on the cover of the ledger.

And now he noticed something very odd, something which for some moments kept him motionless, paralysed with horror.

Under the label on the cover of the ledge he could see the edge of a second label protruding.

He took out his pocket-knife and started scraping the label.

The church-bells were ringing. People were flocking to the church. They had brought out the fire-engine garlanded with flowers. Standing up on the driver's box was Unteroffizier Zobelmann, in top-hat and tails, waving to the populace in a friendly manner.

The village choir was assembling on the main square.

But the bridegroom was sitting crouched in front of the sales ledger, his hair dishevelled, his eyes starting out of his head.

Now he understood all. It was Evelyn who was on the right trail. That was how she had become involved in the espionage affair. He, on the other hand, had been sold the wrong ledger, with the right label pasted on it. It was clear that Grete's Buddha could contain nothing more than a pair of scissors, some embroidery silks, and a few thimbles.

•4•

There was a knock on the door.

Quickly, he hid the book.

"Come in."

It was Uncle Arthur, wearing a frock-coat and a solemn expression.

"Here's your best man, Eddy."

"I couldn't care less. Uncle, I have changed my mind. I don't want the fortune. I am not going to marry this girl. I can't. What can I do?"

"Are you crazy? Just think, my boy, tonight the clay god will be ours!"

"And she'll be mine. No."

"What do you propose to do?"

"Oil out of here."

A.B.C.D. almost foamed at the mouth.

"All right. I will stay! I'll carry on on my own."

"Will you marry her?"

"I will," Arthur Bede said resolutely.

Eddy was deeply moved.

"Oh, uncle. Many's the time you have accused me of being frivolous and cynical. Now you will realize that you were wrong. Have it your own way. I'll let you have the diamond all for yourself and renounce my claim to Grete's hand." He heaved a deep sigh and gazed wistfully out of the window, towards the distant summits. "May you be happy with her."

"You renounce your share?" Rancing the Elder asked.

"I do," replied Rancing the Younger. "All I want you to do is to pay me for my trouble in finding the treasure for you. Give me two thousand quid, and I'll be off."

"Not a penny more!"

"I've no intention of bargaining with you. Wollishoff would give me as much in return for the secret. Maybe more."

He grabbed his hat, flung his overcoat over his arm, and moved to the door.

"Wait! You scoundrel! You blood-sucker!"

"You are really rather ungrateful. For a paltry two thousand quid, I have made you a millionaire. I don't want your sordid money. I'm going to see old Wollishoff!"

"Wait!.. Come, Eddy, why be so touchy? Am I right in thinking that for two thousand pounds sterling you will waive all your rights? Are you ready to sign a statement to that effect?"

"That's right. I don't want to have anything to do with either the diamond or the girl any more."

An hour later, Eddy was on his way to Zürich, whence he proceeded to Marseilles by the very next plane. He was now in possession of a clue of which the police were ignorant. He had only to discover where Lord Bannister lived and there he would find Evelyn. It would, of course, have been possible to pick up a hundred thousand francs right away by handing over this information to the police, but he had no desire to betray her. Besides, he still wanted to get hold of the diamond.

Meantime, Arthur B.C.D. Rancing had explained to old Herr Wollishof that he, too, had fallen in love with Grete, and that he had spent the previous evening persuading his nephew that it would be a great tragedy to deprive a man in the prime of life of his last great love. They had drawn lots and he, Arthur Rancing, had won. His nephew Edward had left for Hüttliberg, broken-hearted. Now he had come on the morning of this festival day to ask for the bride's hand in marriage.

After only a moment's hesitation, Grete happily threw herself into Mr. Arthur Rancing's arms. The girl had already been through two bridal campaigns and was not to be daunted by any unexpected move when a wedding was in view.

"But the banns have not been read," protested the coroner, who was well versed in ecclesiastical law.

"That's all right," said Arthur Bede airily. "They have read out the banns for Mr. Rancing, and that's my name too."

There was a slight commotion among the crowd when it was learned that the chief actor in the drama had been replaced by his uncle but everyone soon accepted the situation. The manager of the local repertory company gave a sizable crowd an account of the bloody duel that had been fought by the two relatives at midnight.

Doctor Loebli, representing the local branch of the First Aid Society, presented to the newly-weds the gift of a silk pillow embroidered with the warning:

Accidents Can Happen To Anyone

•5•

The plane was nearing Morocco. Evelyn and Lord Bannister exchanged only a few words. She said nothing about the "criminal case". She laughed at herself for being so happy. For what cause had she to be happy? When they arrived, they would go their separate ways. She wondered if he would ever discover how complete was her innocence. What was it Uncle Marius would say? "A woman's honour is like a good tailoring: It must not strike the eye, not even to earn praise."

"I say, Lord Bannister," said Holler who, now that he was no longer air-sick, was pestering them with his company once again.

"I wonder when I could have the pleasure of inspecting your laboratory? You did promise that you would show it to me and my editors are waiting eagerly for an article on the subject."

"Ah...er...it's quite up to you. The pleasure will be mine."

"Well, the sooner the better. People in England are tremendously interested in your work. Excuse me."

He made a hurried retreat, for they had begun to come down in a wide spiral, a manoeuvre which always affected him unpleasantly. A few seconds later there was a gentle bump on the ground, the humming noise subsided, the plane taxied up to the hangars, and the long trip was over.

They were in Morocco.

"We must leave in the same taxi," Lord Bannister told Evelyn.

"Let me know where I can drop you on the way. We need only keep up this farce till we've got rid of this horrible Holler. I believe he's leaving us now."

A well-known psychologist tells us that unjustified optimism is a characteristic of most research scientists; and Lord Bannister's present hope that Holler was about to take his leave of them was quite unwarranted. After hailing a taxi, he turned round to say good-bye to the journalist, who, however, did not take his proffered hand, but instead handed his suitcase to the driver.

"With your permission, I will avail myself of your generous invitation and come along with you. One can never afford to miss a good story for the paper, and since Lord Bannister has left it to me to name the time of my visit, my respect for him forbids me to keep him waiting. I hope I am not intruding upon you?"

Well, the Press, as Lord Bannister was well aware, was a formidable taskmaster. The only satisfactory way of dealing with a fellow like this, he thought, would be to mince him up for sausages. He cursed the habit of casual politeness which had driven him to invite Holler to chose the time of his visit; there was nothing for it now but to grin and bear it.

He wondered if this Nosey Parker could possibly have any suspicion about the real nature of their situation.

Now he would be compelled to take the girl with him to his villa, to keep up appearances. She came to his assistance.

"I shall go straight into town. I have a number of things to attend to rather urgently."

"In that case I shall not stay long, for I would be only too happy to serve as your guide, Lady Bannister."

'Why ever don't people like this bounder get run over by trams while they are still children?' reflected Lord Bannister moodily before saying aloud:

"I will have luncheon served immediately."

"That will be nice," Evelyn replied sadly. "I feel hungry."

Lord Bannister was aware that she was both hungry and tired, and that he had no wish to drop her somewhere in the street. But what was the explanation of his reluctance? It was high time to part company with Evelyn Weston, the girl with a price on her head—alive or dead!

And here he was taking her home with him—alive! And hungry!

Lord Bannister' villa was in the wealthiest residential district of Guéliz and was set in a flowery garden screened from view by the dense foliage of palm trees.

Luncheon was not a very cheerful meal although P. J. Holler tucked in and laughed heartily at his own jokes. Evelyn found it hard to realize that she was in Africa. The dining-room might have been in London: there was even a fireplace. She looked round rather wistfully, touching the prayer rug, and picking up a porcelain shepherdess from the mantelpiece. She quietly came to the conclusion that it was going to be painful to leave this place—something she would have to do pretty soon.

She did not notice when Lord Bannister and his visitor left the dining-room to go to the laboratory. A beckoning armchair brought home to her the fact that she had had practically no sleep for the last twenty-four hours. Sadly, she put on her hat, slipped quietly out of the house and hurried down the garden path. She closed the lattice gate behind her.

·6·

She hesitated for a few moments, wondering where to start looking first, then she hailed a taxi and told the driver to take her to the top of the hill where the fortress of Guéliz was situated. The soldiers at the reception office received her politely. A sick legionary? Münster?... Well, what was the nature of the business she wished to discuss with him?... A family affair?... H'm... The men here seldom had family affairs, though this... er... Münster might well be an exception. Perhaps she would make inquiries at the garrison hospital.

But no, *Légionnaire* Münster was not at the hospital at the moment. He had received treatment here recently. Where was he now? Well, *madame* would understand that they must supply no information without permission from the Commanding Officer. She had come from there? Well, would she kindly go back there and go straight to the Paymaster's office, Number Two Company, Reserve Battalion H. Q. So she returned to Guéliz.

"Sorry, *madame*," said the sentry. "The office is closed now. Anyway, the Reserve Battalion H.Q. Paymaster's office can give no information on postings of anyone serving in the ranks unless specially instructed to do so by the central Regimental Command of G.H.Q., Oran, and for this they must have written permission from the Commanding Officer. That's all you need. With a bit of luck—and influence—the rest goes like clockwork."

That was all she had accomplished by 1 p.m. She had been so intent on her mission that she had not noticed that she was being shadowed by a man with a full beard.

Once again she found herself standing in the centre of the town, dispirited, and wondering where she could go to next. There was no one to whom she could turn for help for she herself was wanted by the police—alive or dead. Suddenly, a familiar voice spoke behind her.

"Oh, hel-lo!" said the voice. "Could I escort you anywhere, Lady Bannister?"

It was Holler! He was the man she needed!

"Hello. Have you finished your interview with... er... my husband?" She blushed. My *husband*, forsooth! A pretty humbug she had become.

"Oh, yes. We finished pretty soon. Lord Bannister pressed me to stay longer, but can't stand being cooped up for very long. You look rather tired. Would you care to have tea with me? I should be delighted."

"Thank you." She felt so weak and tired that she accepted the invitation with relief. She decided to ask his advice. After all, there was no one else she could possibly consult.

"Lord Bannister has done an admirable job," Holler enthused over tea. "He showed me one of the cultures. Amazing! Under the microscope it looked like a herd of fine Merino sheep on an alpine pasture. What a germ pen! I don't understand anything about it though. I should have thought he would want to destroy these animals, not cultivate them. But, of course, a newspaperman isn't supposed to know about medicine. The important thing is that Lord Bannister is a popular man, and that every time I run a feature on his sleeping-sickness theory in the Sunday supplement, we get heaps of letters of congratulation."

"I usually cut out those articles," she said cunningly. Her words had an amazing effect.

"Really?" said Holler, his cheeks aglow. "You make me happy, Lady Bannister. Lord Bannister is sometimes dissatisfied with my articles. Finds fault with trifles. Recently, he quite seriously scolded me because, he said, sleeping-sickness and malaria are two different things. Well, I am no physician and how could I be expected to know all the details? The important thing was that the readers talked about the Sunday article for days and that a League of Artisans for Combating Sleeping-Sickness was founded and I was elected Vice-President. Lord Bannister has been elected Honorary President of the League and resolution passed calling for a major consignment of alarm-clocks to be sent to India, for the benefit of people suffering from sleeping-sickness. Thanks to the campaign conducted in my papers, we have managed to rouse people's consciences, and society is at last prepared to combat sleeping-sickness."

"Henry is rather a severe critic in scientific matters."

"It must be a family trait."

"Yes. The Bannisters on the whole are conservative."

"The Bannisters! But I think there is only one Lord Bannister?"

"I mean to say...that is... even though Henry has no brothers..."

Holler looked astounded.

"I understood that he had several brothers!"

She realized how careful she would have to be if she was not to drop a brick and therefore replied boldly, "I see that you are not too well informed about our family."

"Who? Me? I should think I am a walking Debrett. Take Bannister. Your husband's late uncle's father did some renowned work in the classification of warm-blooded mammals of the tertiary period, and in recognition of these services a gracious sovereign was pleased to bestow on him a peerage. He was the first Lord Bannister. The second Lord Bannister was your husband's late uncle. This Lord Bannister, Austin Clifford, the universally esteemed vermicelli-and-noodles manufacturer, died eight years ago, and as he had no children, his title was inherited by your respected husband. As you see, Lady Bannister, a British newspaperman is not wholly ignorant of the noble families of Great Britain. Now, if your marriage should be blessed with a son... Hullo!... Today, something always seems to be down the wrong way either with Lord Bannister or with you. Oh, just let it dry. It leaves no stain."

With difficulty, she recovered from her coughing fit. "You do seem to know the history of our family pretty well."

"You see, that's what's so nice about the English practice of granting titles. You come into this world as a plain Mr. Smith, then if you're lucky some distant relation may die leaving no son, and a plain scientist can inherit both a title and a new name."

"I think perhaps we might ask for the bill, Mr. Holler. I still have some business to settle. I hope this time I shall be successful."

"Can I be of any help to you? I know Morocco inside out. I come over here several times a year, and publish long reports about the horrors of Africa."

"I would like to trace a sick member of the Legion. He used to be a good friend of a cousin of mine and I promised his family in London that I would make inquiries about him here."

"In that case, it's really lucky for you that I am here. The authorities are somewhat unaccommodating when it comes to matters concerning those fellows. You can never tell what people may want to see them about. But I know how to tackle the Commanding Officer...*Garçon!* The bill!"

•7•

Once again, she was in a taxi on the way to Guéliz. This time, however, Holler was sitting by her side.

At the fortress, Holler showed himself in his most boisterous mood. First he quarrelled with the sentry, who again refused admittance on the grounds that the office was closed. Holler spoke so violently that eventually an officer came out and after listening to the journalist, led them into the fort.

By the time they reached the office on the second floor, Holler had made friends with four high-ranking officers and everyone in the office was talking freely. Bestowing ten francs here, a benign smile there, stern with one fellow and all affability with another, he struck the right note everywhere. He took the formidable fortress of Guéliz by storm.

By four o'clock, they had found out that Münster was recovering from a serious wound at no great distance from the fortress, in Number Two Company's convalescent camp in the oasis of Marbouk: a mere two days' ride by camel.

"It's so very good of you," said Evelyn.

Holler beamed happily, and replied:

"Oh, it's nothing. Last year, it took me only two days to trace a leather merchant who hadn't been seen since the Boer War. What do you propose to do now, Lady Bannister?"

Evelyn wished he would be less of a stickler for address. Every other sentence of this title-maniac made the blush rise to her cheeks.

"I shall make the trip to Oasis Marbouk. I've never been to a place like that anyway."

"Will Lord Bannister go with you?"

"N-no...For once, I'd like to go on my own. I don't want to disturb him in his work. Can you hire guides here, do you know?"

"Certainly. Have you not yet made a trip into the desert?"

"No, I haven't. That's just the idea..."

"But then you won't have the necessary equipment, either. Now isn't this sheer luck that I am here! I have been to the Sahara lots of times. And without spending much money either. And yet these merchant robbers will skin you if you don't look out. Will you permit me to arrange your trip for you?"

"I don't know how to thank you..."

"It'll be pleasure. In the first place, the equipment. For, you see, skirts and that sort of thing are useless a few hundred yards south of the town. However, I'm not going to take you to any of the bazaars in the centre of the town. What you want is an Arab merchant. None but Arabs. In the centre, they will sell you inferior goods at high prices, though they behave so politely. Let the tourists go to those shops... Taxi!"

He took Evelyn to Mellah. In the tumult of the *marché arabe,* they could only move forward inch by inch. Having reached what appeared to be the narrowest alley in the most squalid part of the Arab quarter, Holler dismissed the taxi and they proceeded on foot down the evil-smelling lane.

They did not notice the man with the full beard who from time to time spat out bits of tobacco and who had followed them all the way from the camp.

Holler took Evelyn into a small, dimly lit shop, which was buzzing with flies. The shopkeeper, a hawk-nosed Arab with a goatee, emerged from the semi-darkness to greet them. Then they selected everything that was needed—topee, topboots, breeches, thermos flask, food-box sealed hermetically with a rubber tape, and the rest of the paraphernalia.

Next came bargaining, such as Evelyn had never seen before.

At first the merchant laughed; later on, he beat his chest, rushed into the street and shook his fists at the passers-by. After that, he came rushing back, foaming at the mouth, and tugging and tearing at his burnous; then, throwing up his hands, he gazed despairingly at the ceiling before throwing himself on the breeches, sobbing as if he was mourning over the body of his son. Holler, on the other hand, beat the table with one fist, then laughed sardonically, and seemed to be trying to prove something by rolling up one leg of his trousers to show the merchant the quality of his sock. The merchant was visibly impressed and pushed the sun-helmet over to Holler; but when the latter reached for the breeches, he once again went berserk, like a bitch when someone tries to get near her pup, and clasped the garment to his bosom, breathing heavily.

An hour later, all the things lay before them on the counter, neatly wrapped. They paid, and left.

"You have made an excellent bargain," Holler said, wiping the perspiration from his forehead contentedly.

"Aren't you afraid that this Arab will kill you one day?"

"What! This man? Why, I'm one of his regular customers. He is a good friend of mine. We write to each other when I am in London."

•8•

With the guide, it was smoother sailing. These were desert people, well-organized.

The guide was a short, scraggy Berber, with dark-brown skin and curly hair round his shaven crown. He said that if they set out at dawn next day they might arrive at Marbouk during the morning of the fourth day.

"Could I go with him across the desert at night?" Evelyn asked Holler.

"You will be absolutely safe with me, madam," replied the Berber in impeccable English. " Desert guides are true-blue gentlemen."

She felt ashamed.

"These fellows are just great children," Holler said, laughing. "I knew a Berber guide who worked for years with the Philadelphia Concert Orchestra and eventually returned to the desert because of a disappointment in love."

A chocolate-coloured little girl came out of the house to admire the lovely European lady at close quarters.

"What a sweet darling," Evelyn said. She lifted the child from the dust, and wiped the smudged little face. Then she gave the little one her brooch which in fact was of no value and served only to fasten her shawl.

"An amulet," the little one stammered, amazed. "A charm!" The child hardly dared touch the shining object.

"They will go though fire and water for you now," Holler explained to her as they walked away. "Well, good-bye to you. I hope you will succeed. Be sure to arrive punctually at the appointed place. These guides are apt to turn round and go home if the fare isn't there on time."

CHAPTER NINE. *Lord Bannister suffers from hallucinations. He is then mistaken for Catherine de Medici. He prepares for his impending years in prison, then discovers that dinner jackets aren't the most comfortable wear in the Sahara. Robbers make their appearance. Eddy Rancing rides his camel full tilt, and learns to appreciate the theory of relativity.*

•1•

Evelyn was punctual. Dressed in her new travelling outfit, she arrived at the appointed place at the appointed time. Before setting out, she scribbled a hasty note which she handed to a messenger, instructing him to take it to Lord Bannister; then she climbed into the saddle of the kneeling camel.

Azrim, the Berber guide, uttered a strange strident guttural sound, whereupon the camels rose in two separate swinging movements. Evelyn thought first, that she was being ejected from her saddle and would fall on her face; then, that she was being catapulted backwards. When at last she reached an erect position, she found herself at an alarming height.

"Reg-lak! Reg-lak!"

The camels broke into a trot.

•2•

Only twelve hours previously, a much bigger caravan had departed along the same route: it consisted of thirty Arabs, handpicked gems of Mellah, headed by the two leaders, Adams and Gordon, who had become great friends.

The gang had arrived from Lyons by chartered plane and had immediately dispersed in search of the girl, having divided the town into sectors among themselves. Rainer was left to act as liaison in the lobby of the Hotel Mammunia, where the hoary killer picked up the manager of a European engineering firm, and before long the two of them were playing chess.

It was Yoko, the man with the full beard, whose efforts were crowned with success. He had started from the assumption that, as the girl was looking for a soldier, she was certain to call on the Commanding Officer of the fortress. He therefore concealed himself in the neighbourhood of Fort Guéliz, where he soon spotted Evelyn. From there, he tailed her for the rest of the afternoon until she checked in at the Hotel de Paris to have a rest.

Yoko then returned to the Berber guide whom he had seen talking with the girl, for he knew that he must discover what place Evelyn Weston was bound for.

"*Salaam,*" Yoko greeted the Berber.

"*Bonjour,*" said the man.

"I want to make a longish trip in the Sahara, but I must start without delay, and I am looking for a reliable guide."

"I am sorry, Sir," replied the Berber. "I have been hired for five days."

As he spoke these words he remembered the British lady, and, with a smile about his lips, watched the flushed and happy child playing with the amulet.

"Perhaps you could merge the two caravans," Yoko suggested.

"I want to go to Ain Sefra; and if your people are going that way..."

All unsuspecting, the guide told Yoko just what he wanted to know.

"We are going in another direction—to the Oasis Marbouk."

"Too bad. *Salaam aleikum.*"

"*Au revoir.*"

Yoko had learned what he wanted. Since Evelyn was preparing to go to the Oaasis Marbouk, it was probable that the wounded soldier "Münster" was to be found there. Quickly, he returned to the hotel to give Rainer this information; the other members of the gang were then recalled, and within an hour, they were holding a conference.

"It's quite simple," said Adams. "We'll ride out ahead today."

He touched the map with one finger. "When Evelyn Weston sets out early tomorrow morning, we'll have reached this well. There we'll lie in wait, take the map from her and then go and see this fellow Münster in the oasis."

"What's public safety in Oasis Marbouk like?" Dr. Cournier butted in in his low-pitched, drowsy, aristocratic voice, beating a slow devil's tattoo with his large freckled white fingers.

"I mean in case we find we can't win the man over by persuasion only."

"We should in any case recruit some thirty or forty Arabs here," the man with the beard said. "I know a landlord in the Quartier Réservé—an old pal of mine. He'll help us. In these desert enterprises you're liable to meet with surprises. I'm all for playing it safe."

Shortly afterwards, Beefy made the acquaintance of an army officer who told him that public safety in Oasis Marbouk was, from the doctor's point of view, pretty encouraging: no police, no soldiers; peace and order, never disturbed in Oasis Marbouk from time immemorial, was maintained by the very small garrison of the little army convalescent camp.

"I think," Adams said in the afternoon, "we can leave within the hour. Everything's been arranged."

"Not everything," Rainer dissented. "We must take a few thermos flasks filled with tea. Tea is a good drink in tropical heat."

No one deigned to answer.

•3•

"In this moment of departure, my grateful thoughts go out to you. God bless you for your kindness. As you will never see me again, I trust you will forget the trouble and inconvenience that were caused to you by the unhappy

Evelyn Weston"

He looked up from the letter and gazed out across the garden. He felt a heaviness pressing on his heart. It seemed that in spite of all the trouble she had brought him he had become dangerously accustomed to the company of this harum-scarum but infinitely sweet girl who was always in such a state of alarm, rushing about and getting excited about her chief enemy—his toilet case. The Blonde Hurricane. She swept through his life, leaving only confusion in her wake, and she herself rushed on into mortal danger. Not that she had so much courage; she was simply reckless.

Her departure had certainly brought him one great blessing—the possibility of a quiet night's sleep; and his peace would be no longer disturbed by her abrupt and untimely appearances.

•4•

"Good afternoon. I am looking for Miss Evelyn Weston."

Lord Bannister was taken aback; in fact, he very nearly fainted with surprise.

Standing at the door was a good-looking young man wearing shining top-boots and white breeches and holding in his hand a sun-helmet the size of a car-wheel—in a word, he was wearing the tropical kit seen only on film stars and members of escorted tours commonly seen in Venice and along the Adriatic coast; but here in the tropics tourists who sport the latest Sahara fashion are more conspicuous; they are also figures of fun, for their fashionable garb is an open invitation to sunstroke.

"Wh-who are you?" Lord Bannister stammered with misgiving.

"My name is Edward Rancing. Am I speaking to Lord Bannister?"

"Cerainly... yes... Er... Why do you ask?"

"I am looking for Miss Evelyn Weston. I should like to speak to her."

His lordship's eyes wandered vaguely about the room as if to say that he had just put her down somewhere recently, but didn't remember where. Then he came to his senses and drew himself up.

"I don't quite see what I can do for you, Mr. Rancing."

"I should have thought I'd made it sufficiently clear. I am looking for Miss Evelyn Weston. She was last photographed in your company, Lord Bannister."

Lord Bannister cowered once more, shinking visibly. Eddy produced a photograph from his pocket.

"I think this is an authentic photograph. I am informed that you arrived here with this lady, ostensibly your wife; it seems reasonable, therefore, to come to you to discover the whereabouts of Miss Evelyn Weston."

"Are you a detective?" asked Lord Bannister, as devious as any pickpocket playing hide-and-seek with the police.

"Oh, no. I am an old acquaintance of Miss Weston's. I have been her next-door neighbour in the King's Road for some years."

"I suppose it's not merely a neighbourly action of yours to have followed Miss Weston to Africa?" Lord Bannister observed moodily.

"No. I would like to see her on business."

"Now which country are *you* spying for?"

"Me? For Lappland."

"By gad, sir, do you mean to say you have come all the way to Africa disguised as an opera chorus-singer just to tell me bad jokes?"

"It's no more of a joke than your question, Lord Bannister."

"After all that's been written in the papers..."

"I have been Miss Weston's next-door neighbour for several years. She lives in great penury with her widowed mother. She is an honest, hard-working person and I am quite sure that she has been innocently involved in this horrible affair."

All this was news to Lord Bannister. So she was no spy, after all.

"That's all very well," he said at last. "Nevertheless, I haven't the faintest idea where Miss Weston may be now. All I can tell you is that she won't come back here anymore."

Eddy smiled sarcastically.

"I am sure Miss Weston will come back. I'm not going to stir from here till she does."

"As I have no desire to spend my remaining years in your company I shall be compelled to..."

"Go to the police? All right. That'll mean a hundred thousand francs for me. For you, it will most likely mean jail."

That was a possibly Lord Bannister had not anticipated and he fell back limply into his chair. Fate was against him. He might have guessed that girl would land him in jail.

"I don't want to pester you, Lord Bannister. All I ask is that you will allow me to remain."

"What else can I do? I must behave like a gentleman. Please take a seat."

Eddy sat down and proceeded to mix himself a drink from some bottles that stood on the table. When he spoke again it was in a more light-hearted and friendly tone.

"Have you really married Miss Weston?"

"I haven't. As I found out in the end, I had only been protecting her. There was always someone following the poor girl, and whenever she found out she would come and wake me up and then fall asleep herself. So far her plan has worked very well. And you say you are no accomplice of hers?"

"Miss Weston, I repeat, is a decent middle-class girl."

"She lives rather a rough-and-tumble life to be that."

"She is searching for her lawful inheritance."

"I know. Also a certain gentleman's honour. I can assure you, if you are interested, that she and I have been quite active in both matters. Well, do you seriously plan to stay with me from now on?"

"I do. But I won't be here for long. I firmly believe that Miss Weston will soon be back."

"You are, it seems, an English Nostradamus. Though it is a historical fact that even that illustrious gentleman made some mistakes now and then."

"I am not mistaken. You will soon realize that I am right."

"But I shall have to pay rather a high price for the realization," replied Lord Bannister ruefully.

"Never mind. If I am Nostradamus, you should look upon yourself as Catherine de Medici and sacrifice something so that my prediction will come true."

"Mr. Rancing, I give you my word that I have been speaking the truth. You may call me a scoundrel and a cad if Miss Evelyn Weston ever comes back to his house."

"Well," replied Eddy, with a sigh, "with all respect, I have the honour to inform your lordship that your lordship is a scoundrel and a cad."

Evelyn Weston was standing at the door.

·5·

For several hours Evelyn and her guides made their way through the desert. Eastwards they could see crumbling stone pillars and torsos—ruins of an ancient city dating from the time of the Roman conquest. Then Evelyn accidentally tore her coat and in order to prevent it from tearing further, she decided to mend it immediately. For this purpose she opened her small black case.

"Good gracious! Where's the envelope?" was her horrified exclamation.

Inside the case lay a folded towel, flanked, on either side, by a clothes-brush and a cake of soap. It was her old enemy, Lord Bannister's toilet case! Once again they had each picked up the other's case. Now it was Lord Bannister who had the orange-coloured envelope with him! What was she to do?

There was nothing for it but to turn back! Lord Bannister was in mortal peril. What would happen if he opened the case in the presence of other people, and found the envelope? He might even hand it over to the police.

Oh, how she longed to dash the case to the ground, along with that hateful shaving kit which it no doubt contained. Yet now she would have to take it back to him if she wanted to exchange it for her own.

"Azrim! We must turn back! Quick! We must return immediately."

·6·

She was standing on the doorstep. But the fresh surprise which greeted her there robbed her of speech. How on earth had Edward Rancing come to be here? Dimly she began to make out the outlines of a confused and fantastic story. Her head was swimming as if she had drunk too much wine.

"Mr. Rancing!"

"Hullo, Miss Weston," said Eddy, smiling. "How nice to see you again."

Lord Bannister dared not speak. Gradually, his surprise gave way to alarm. Her reappearance must herald an approaching storm. In the midst of the dead calm, she had arrived mysteriously, a hurricane; and she would disappear again in the same silent mysterious fashion, leaving wreckage everywhere in her wake.

Alarm sirens began to wail in Lord Bannister's mind. It was quite certain, he decided, that she was being followed, that robbers were lying in wait of her, and that before long she would insist on his joining her on some long and inconvenient trip. And so he hurriedly filled his pockets with cigarettes, and took from his wardrobe a warm comforter. He had better be somewhat prepared.

"What... How on earth did you get here?" she asked Rancing.

"Why should he know that, of all people?" Lord Bannister mused sadly. "Nothing strange about that. The only thing that's to be wondered at is the fact that I am still here. Where are we going to?" he asked Evelyn rather anxiously.

"For once I am not going to drag you along with me on my uncomfortable errand."

"May those words prove to be a prophecy. I have lost my faith in miracles like that."

"With your permission, I would like to accompany you," Eddy butted in.

Lord Bannister cast a nervous sideways glance in his direction.

"I am glad to see," he said turning to Evelyn, "that neighbourly solidarity is so strong in the King's Road."

For a second she scrutinised Lord Bannister's face searchingly. Oh, dear, was it possible that he was being jealous?

"I wish you would express yourself more clearly, Mr. Rancing. What do you expect me to do for you?"

"I offer you my services. I have an idea that in the present situation you need the assistance of a man. With my help, you may be able to recover the heirloom more quickly."

"How do you come to know anything about my inheritance?"

"Miss Weston! You will despise me. I was eavesdropping."

"And what is your next move? You know everything; you know that I am being followed, and that I am looking for something that's worth a fortune. So you propose to blackmail me? Is that it?"

"Shall I be frank with you? I was thinking of doing that. But somehow, I can't. Miss Weston, I feel like a naughty boy caught by a kind and aged teacher. I suppose I respect you, and this sentiment has been known to kill many a resolution at the very moment when action was necessary. I would like the chance to play out this gamble to the end. But I am not going to blackmail you. If you won't take me with you, I will go away."

"And go to the police, of course," she said sarcastically, "to denounce me."

"Miss Weston," protested Eddy, deeply hurt, and his blushes revealed Edward F.G.H. Rancing, the genius, for what he really was—a great child. "Miss Weston, you are doing me an injustice. I could have done that before. I am a frivolous sort of fellow; I love money; but this time I really wanted to get hold of your inheritance so that I would be able to bring it to you and ask you to marry me."

Evelyn burst out laughing.

"Oh, all right, Eddy. I suppose you'll just never sober down. You *are* a madcap. All right, then. I have nothing against your joining me. I *have* been very much left to my own devices, so far. I've had nobody by my side."

"Mainly," said Lord Bannister, trying to justify himself before Eddy," because the night-shirt I was wearing was so conspicuous that I was compelled to sit in the back of my car on the floor."

"That's all over now. You will not be asked to make any more inconvenient trips on my behalf."

"Miss Weston, you have said that so many times. I believe we are in God's hand, all of us."

"Well, I am about to explain to you that it is my intention to leave you here in peace and never ask you for anything again."

She was a lovely girl, Lord Bannister thought. The trouble was that you simply couldn't tell when she was going to change into a hurricane.

"I have come back because we have the wrong cases again. I've brought back this hateful toilet case of yours. I just took a glance at the contents, and slammed the lid on them all. Here you are!" She threw the case down on the table with so much disgust that inside the Buddha's belly, the blades and the shaving block positively danced together. "Now I will thank you to give me back my own case. Then Eddy and I will go away and you will have seen the last of us."

"It's nice to know that in the King's Road the neighbours use Christian names to each other—a custom prevalent in the rest of England only among relatives or very good friends."

With this acid remark, Lord Bannister crossed over to the fireplace and took the small case from the mantelpiece.

"But this *is* my case," he said. "Are you sure you're not mistaken, Miss Weston?" With a practiced gesture he opened the lid of the case.

Three heads turned to look, three mouths opened in amazement, and three hearts missed a beat.

Just inside the case they could see the orange-coloured envelope with the five seals.

·7·

Evelyn walked resolutely towards the case.

However, Lord Bannister closed it, and slowly placed his hand over it with the lazy, possessive movement of a lion when she curls her paw over a piece of meat, staking a claim to possession.

"Give me my case, please," she said nervously.

"You may have your case, of course; but I am afraid I can't let you take the envelope. Until now, I have ignored the information which has come to my ears. Unfortunately however, as things are at present, the envelope would have to pass through my hands to reach you, and later, your employers. In which case I should become just as much of an intelligence agent as, say, Mata Hari."

Evelyn reflected. It was true Lord Bannister had until now played only a passive role in the affair. And it was equally true that by handing the envelope to her he would become her accomplice. Lord Bannister an intelligence agent! A prospective candidate for the Nobel Prize, a celebrated scientist and—what made it even more impossible to contemplate—a gentleman with very high moral standards.

"You realize, don't you, Miss Weston, that you are asking the impossible of an old-fashioned scientist when you expect him to hand over this letter to you? However, I promise to let you get a good start and escape before I hand in this document."

Eddy Rancing was toying with the neck of the whisky bottle as if only waiting for a sign from the girl to hit Lord Bannister over the head with it and thus close this whole painful argument. But Evelyn gave him not the slightest encouragement.

She made some silent calculations while Lord Bannister watched her anxiously. At last she came out with her tentative suggestion.

"Do you think," she asked, "that it would be too much trouble for you to make a longish trip by camel?"

"That's just what I've been expecting," Lord Bannister replied dejectedly.

•8•

The first minor blast of the hurricane caught at his nerves. Her eyes were shining bright as she turned over various plans in her mind and there was no doubt about it: she was intending to make full use of the famous but defenceless student of sleeping-sickness.

"You plan to hand in this envelope to the authorities, don't you?"

"I do. But I don't propose to deliver it by camel. I shall go on foot. For some time past, I have had a morbid aversion to all forms of transport, if you know what I mean."

"If you want to hand it in here in Morocco, we will go to the police together. But I wonder if the humane spirit of a true-born English gentleman permits him to deny his assistance to a defenceless woman and an innocent man whose name has been dragged through the mud."

"You have already used that excuse for dragging me halfway across Europe—first in tails and later in my nightshirt."

"This time it's only to a nearby oasis."

"That's what you say at this moment. But once we are on our way, we may find it impossible to stop, however much we would like to do so, till we get to Cape Town. To say nothing of the fact that a camel is no motor-car; it has no replaceable spare parts and if any part detached, we shall be stuck in the desert."

"I wish you would stop being sarcastic. We can travel with a heavy escort. It's only two days' ride by camel. You may keep the document and you need not part with it unless you are satisfied that it will get into the hands of the right person. If you refuse to do this you will be sacrificing for the sake of your own convenience the rightful inheritance of a poor family and the honour of a man who has been wronged."

He felt the blast of the hurricane lifting him up and sucking him in—he had no more strength to resist.

"Can you give me any reasonable explanation? Can you prove what you have been telling me?"

"I can bear out the greater part of her story," said Eddy.

"And I can explain everything else. In the first place, this is..."

"Wait! Lord Bannister interrupted. "Don't tell me anything. I want to preserve my ignorance of the facts. After all that I've read about it, I am afraid I should hardly be in a position to place myself at your disposal if you acquainted me with the facts. My position at the moment is like this. I consider that you have entrusted me with this envelope and have asked me to hand it over to authorities not here but at Oasis Marbouk. I intend to comply with your request. We'd better stick to that, I think. In this way, my conscience is, in a way, quite clear. You have, to my great regret, invested me with so much power that I dare not refuse. Let me warn you, however, that beyond the Sahara there is the Belgian Congo, and that nothing—neither your inheritance nor the honour of my fellow-men nor the knowledge that you are being followed—will induce me to follow you there. I won't go farther than the Sahara!"

Evelyn looked at him sorrowfully.

"Are you sure, Lord Bannister?"

Lord Bannister hesitated—and was lost.

"Well, you... er... would have to supply some very powerful reasons," he said in an uncertain voice. "But even if I did go as far as, say the Congo... I would on no account go farther than Cape Town... I mean to say... er... Ah, all right. Let's go."

Perched on the hump of a camel, Lord Bannister had the sullen air of an officer in command of a punitive expedition. Nor was his temper improved by the presence of a great variety of biting and stinging insects which the camel harboured on its body and which made forays to collect his own blood like so many research workers studying sleeping-sickness. He nodded jerkily along to the rhythm of the animal's gait, reflecting bitterly that once again his kind-heartedness had involved him in an uncomfortable journey to defend other people's honour and good name. The truth was very much simpler.

He was following a pretty woman—a little priggishly perhaps, but nevertheless obeying man's eternal law of gravity. He was following her meaninglessly and hopelessly, into the Sahara. But because he was an English peer and a scientist, he liked to justify what he was doing and make his actions seem less humiliating. He was, in fact, doing nothing more and nothing less than one might expect in such circumstances from, say, an enamoured haberdasher.

"Reg-lak! Reg-lak!

The camel broke into a canter, tossed back its head, and gave Lord Bannister such a shaking that he began to cough and splutter helplessly.

"Reg-lak! Reg-lak!"

After a few more blows in the chest from the camel, he managed to sit upright in the saddle, and this position made him feel strong and authoritative once more.

•9•

On this particular journey we have to record that Eddy Rancing's powers of endurance did not equal those of Lord Bannister, in spite of the fact that he was much younger. He soon realized that it is not for nothing that camels have been called 'ships of the desert': the undulating movement of the animal he was riding induced in him symptoms that most decidedly resembled sea-sickness. Then too, the dust made his eyes sting so painfully that he could scarcely bear it and there were moments when Eddy felt that he was at the end of his tether.

Evelyn, on the other hand, had had some practice in steeling herself against sea-sickness. Besides, women usually manage to endure the hardships of the tropics more equably than men and she was therefore riding along by the side of the guide in relatively good cheer.

The sun's rays began to lengthen and between the softly contoured sand-dunes stretching away on every side, there appeared tiny shadows, turning the desert into a vast chessboard with alternating squares of light and dark.

Lord Bannister stroked his chin moodily.

"I forgot to shave," he muttered, but broke off as he caught the girl's eye.

She glimpsed the toilet case he had tied between the two goatskins on the water-bearing camel! When they arrived at the oasis he would doubtless retire to a room and shave! Angrily, she hoped he would have to walk about with half an inch of stubble on his chin for the next few days.

As for her own case, she never stopped clutching it.

The desert, where the sand was mingled with the dusty bones of so many people who had been assassinated according to the rules of vendetta, infected Evelyn with the idea of merciless revenge.

She made up her mind to pay off old scores by getting rid of that toilet case for good. She would let the shifting sands of the Sahara swallow up that nuisance of a toilet kit, soap, brush, blades and all.

Much as Othello must have edged his way towards Desdemona's bed so now Evelyn stealthily approached the water-bearing camel, allowing Lord Bannister and the guide to ride ahead. Presently, the treacherous knife flashed, and the leather strap groaned as it was slashed by the blade. There was only a slight thud as the impudent little case dropped into the dust muffling the painful clatter of the clashing toiletware within. Then it was left far behind.

Lord Bannister was preoccupied with his own thoughts and did not notice the incident. Evelyn glanced back. She alone could see that tiny, immobile speck in the distance...

Thus the toilet case was left in the desert—and inside the case was the "Dreaming Buddha" within which there was a diamond worth one million pounds sterling.

·10·

"Reg-lak! Reg lak!"

"We aren't following the normal route, Mademoiselle," said Azrim, the Berber guide.

"Why?"

"It was Allah's will that you gave my daughter an amulet. He has therefore preserved you from grave peril by mixing up your cases and thus causing you to turn back. In this way I learned at home that a lot of bad people were hired in Mellah last night. They have now pitched camp by the desert well, along the caravan route to Marbouk. There is among them a man who yesterday spoke with me and deceived me: he learned from me that you were preparing to go to Marbouk."

Evelyn nearly tumbled down from her saddle.

"I have an idea that those people intend to intercept you by the well, and rob you. But we will make a detour and by-pass them by going through the *shott*. That's what they call the great salt swamp. It is no longer that way, but the route is a bad one and somewhat dangerous. Still, I should think it's better than death."

The end of the conversation was overheard by Lord Bannister and Eddy.

"Well, they've found me," Evelyn said, almost in tears.

"Who are these people?" asked Lord Bannister.

"A group of intelligence agents and gangsters. They are the men whom the police tried to catch when they made the big raid in Paris."

Lord Bannister reflected.

"Do you seriously intend to hand over the envelope to the proper authorities in Marbouk?"

"Yes, I do."

"And can you face the police with a clear conscience when the matter of the envelope has been cleared up?"

"Certainly."

"Right," Lord Bannister nodded. "In that case we must act like honourable citizens. We must give the police this information so that they can run this gang of dangerous criminals to earth by the desert well on the road to Marbouk."

They looked at him in surprise.

"Once you have handed in the envelope," Lord Bannister explained, "and have nothing more to fear, there is no reason why these enemies of society should not be incarcerated in the place where they belong. Mr. Rancing cannot in any case support all this hardship; on the other hand, I have become hardened in Miss Weston's company; therefore I believe the best idea would be for you, Mr. Rancing, to turn back and inform the police of what has come to our knowledge."

Eddy had no objection to his plan, especially as Evelyn declared that she would appreciate that service just as much as if he were to come with her all the way to Marbouk.

"You can't miss the route," said Azrim. "Ride straight ahead with your back to the setting sun. By evening, you will be in sight of the Great Atlas and from there on you'll have something to guide you."

Eddy took leave of the party, and, cooked tender in his picturesque costume, turned his camel for the return journey, his back to the setting sun…

The rest of the party trotted on, forcing the pace as much as their strength permitted. In the blood-red and violet lights of the westering sun the shadows between the sand dunes looked quite black. The heat of the dust-filled air was stifling, and as they advanced, the sulphurous stench of the putrid salt swamp was wafted more and more heavily towards them.

•11•

Eddy urged his camel into a steady canter. The heat was intense, his eyes had become inflamed, he was aching in every limb, and he felt both sick and giddy. But he remembered the appalling day spent in Mügli am See, and the thought that he was away from it all kept him in the saddle.

Conditions here in the Sahara were a good deal better than there, he reflected. By now, Uncle Arthur must either have gone out of his mind or committed suicide. He wondered which. He would have enjoyed seeing what happened after the wedding. There must eventually have arrived the moment when Her Excellency Yakihashi (this was the name Eddy had bestowed on old Wollishoff's so-often-betrothed daughter), presumably with eyes cast down, and wearing one of those amazingly broad smiles, retired to the nuptial bedroom.

And then—ah then, Uncle Arthur would have seized the statuette!

Eddy imagined him stealing quietly away with it to the remotest corner of the park, cautiously avoiding the basement windows behind which Frau Victoria, Head Gardener Krüttikofer's spouse, might be whiling away her time, possibly with Herr Maxl, author of *Wilhelm Tell,* who would doubtlessly be instructing her on some aspect of the drama. At last, at last, would come the long-awaited moment when, by the light of a torch, he would knock the "Dreaming Buddha" sharply against the rim of the fountain.

Eddy saw the Buddha break into fragments; he imagined the contents one by one as each item fell from the little enamelled box, the scissors, thimbles, and thread…and he saw Uncle Arthur rummaging among the débris…looking, and looking, but in vain…

Eddy shuddered, and the Sahara seemed to him at that moment a most desirable place to be in!

That was relativity for you! Inflammation of the eyes and 140 deg. Fahrenheit was bliss when compared with marriage to Grete.

The sun sank and now the desert could be seen in all the beauty of a starry African night.

CHAPTER TEN. *The beard of Achilles. The robbers have no defence against a foul trick. Eddy Rancing discovers that the desert isn't all beer and skittles. He is laughed at by a quite diminutive pilgrim. Lessons from Harrington's daughter stand him in good stead. We learn the lamentable fact that there is scarcely any difference between a razor blade and a self-loading pistol. The toilet case has the last laugh. The fight is over, all are friends and they plan to return a dressing-gown to its rightful owner. Evelyn forgives all. Mr. Bradford, weighing his words carefully, tells us what life is really like.*

·1·

For twenty-four hours the Adams–Gordon Consolidated Co., as the big bloated doctor had nicknamed their gang, had been encamped together with thirty Arab desperadoes beneath the stunted palm-trees of the desert well.

All the gangsters except Rainer had been to the tropics before; and he had taken every precaution to ensure that he would survive all discomforts. His camel positively rustled with paper parcels. Before their departure from the Sahara, he had made numbers of purchases—all kinds of drugs and preventives, from Aspirins to insect-powders and emollients for saddles. He wore green sunglasses and as he rode, held a parasol above his head.

As soon as they had pitched camp, he rubbed himself with some ointment against mosquitoes, and the resulting aroma was so offensive that the other members of the caravan were compelled to pitch their tents at a safe distance from him, and the tethered camels tugged wildly at the ropes.

After one hour, several of the party took down their tents and pitched them at an even greater distance from Rainer who, however, was not offended; he knew that they were too ignorant to be aware of the dangers against which he was protecting himself, malaria, yellow fever and the sleeping-sickness carried by mosquitoes. Doctor Cournier, however, was curious to know the composition of an anti-mosquito ointment with such a horrible smell, and he looked at the bottle lying by Rainer's side. He read on the label:

CAMEL GREASE

Rub injured hoof generously. Isolate animal so as to keep air inside stable from becoming tainted with penetrating smell of ointment.

HOOVES NEED TO BE TAKEN CARE OF!

"I think," Adams said to Gordon, "we'd better drop the idea of trying to sound out this fellow Brandon-Münster. Much better to raid the oasis with our thirty men, capture the bloke and grill him about the Buddha."

"Unless something crops up to prevent us," the doctor remarked.

"There he goes again, the old pessimist," snarled Beefy, who even in the desert wore a dinner-jacket and had also swathed a green ribbon round his sun-helmet.

"You are mistaken. It is not pessimistic to be circumspect," replied the fully qualified poison-retailer reproachfully in his soft, mellifluous voice. He enjoyed little popularity with his collaborators because of his haughty, aristocratic manner. "In my opinion, there's been a little flaw in our scheme. It's an insignificant flaw, but let a single screw work loose and the most complex machine will often break down." He fanned himself with his silk handkerchief: the wind was blowing from Rainer's direction bringing with it a new blast of the overpowering stench. "In my view, the little flaw in our scheme has been the beard of our esteemed friend Yoko."

"I'll thank you not to try to drag me in by my beard," Yoko snorted.

"Come, come," the doctor said, soothingly. "Let's not be touchy now. We have to consider the common interest."

"Very well," said the man with the beard threateningly. "But you'd better consider my beard an Achilles elbow."

"You mean heel, my friend," said the doctor in magisterial tones.

"If I happened to be a doctor," retorted Yoko acrimoniously, "I too would be able to put a name to the various parts of the human body."

"Now, now, my friends, will you kindly shut up," said Adams, calling the litigants to heel. "Or rather let he doctor talk and tell us where he thinks we have gone wrong."

"Eh bien," Dr. Cournier said, "I am afraid we have done the very opposite of what we hoped to do. Yesterday, Mr. Yoko got information from the guide about the Weston girl by pretending that he wanted to go to Ain Sefra. Later on, he accompanied you, Monsieur Gordon, when you hired Arabs for our raid on Marbouk. Yoko has such an ...er... conspicuous exterior that he must have been noticed and people would realise that he intended to go to Marbouk, not Ain Sefra."

"That is possible," Gordon agreed. "Still, it's not likely that anyone found it particularly suspicious or extraordinary."

"That's why I compared this little flaw to a small screw."

Towards the evening of the following day, they began to grow impatient; the victims ought to have arrived by now.

A few Arabs were sent out to reconnoitre. They were told that it was essential for them to discover whether the girl was on the way already. If her party could not be seen anywhere near by, then something had gone wrong.

It was very hot. Everyone gave Rainer a wide berth as if he was a leper, but the unbearable smell of his ointment made their stomachs heave even at a distance of twenty yards. Only the mosquitoes could endure the ointment:

they swarmed round the bespectacled fellow and bit him till the blood spurted.

The patrol returned.

"We have seen their traces," they reported. "We could see the marks left by their camels. They have veered off to the east along a very bad track through the *shott*. Nobody ever uses it."

"Get going, everybody!" Adams cried excitedly.

They broke camp in a matter of minutes. Rainer slipped his crossword puzzle into his pocket, put on his dark sunglasses, and opened his sunshade. He looked like one of the magi.

The camels trotted on as fast as they could and in the first light of dawn a moving speck could be seen in the distance.

"It's a traveller!"

"We'll wait for him," said Gordon; and the gang concealed themselves behind a huge sand dune.

"He is following the tracks made by the party we're after," one of the Arabs said. "He must either have seen them or be one of them."

The traveller approached, prodding his tired camel unsuspectingly towards the great dune.

•2•

Thus it was that in a matter of seconds Eddy Rancing found himself surrounded by a gang of men led by a short, stocky fellow who asked:

"Where are you from?"

Eddy guessed immediately that he was face to face with the gangsters!

"I was heading for Marbouk, but I have had to turn back. My eyes are hurting."

"Did you by any chance meet a woman travelling with one or more companions?"

"No, I didn't."

Gordon laughed.

"So you're one of them. The question was a trap. You are following their track in the reverse direction. Therefore you must have met them. If you deny it you must have a good reason for doing so."

"Let's go!" cried Beefy. "We may overtake them yet!"

"Get rid of this bloke!"

Eddy was aware of an arrow of pain in his head; he saw clusters of gold stars, then fell senseless to the dust.

Beefy had knocked him out with one blow. Then he and Yoko frisked Eddy with lightning speed while Rainer called from the saddle:

"See if he's got some petrol. My lighter's run dry." He put on his pince-nez the better to supervise the search.

"It's just as I have said," purred the creamy voice of Dr. Cournier. "They've found out that we've been hiring men. Yoko's full beard is too conspicuous."

"Listen!" Yoko retorted threateningly. "For the last time I'm warning you to leave my beard out of it. You're just as conspicuous with your impossible dimensions and that crooning voice of yours."

"You ought to take bromide," the doctor suggested.

"Masters!" one of the Arabs butted in. "Now it's quite sure they've taken the road through the *shott*. It's a bad road, and dangerous, but Azrim knows it well. If they turned in that direction yesterday afternoon, we shan't be able to overtake them, for they'll have reached Marbouk tomorrow afternoon, whereas we'll only get there by tomorrow night."

"Now is there any other way of playing foul with gangsters?" Rainer complained indignantly.

"What is the population of Marbouk?" Adams asked.

"A few Arabs—some thirty of them, and their women and children. Then there is a garrison of five soldiers at the sanatorium, and also a few invalid members of the legion."

"It won't take us long to settle them! Let's go!" Gordon exclaimed.

One of the Arabs wanted to shoot Rancing, but the doctor would not allow him.

"Don't do it, my boy," he said in his kindliest tones. "He'll die anyway. Take away his camel and that'll do. If we should get nabbed, a trifle like that can make several years' difference."

Then they all trotted away, leaving Eddy Rancing spreadeagled on the sand as if trying to embrace the entire Sahara.

•3•

Azrim led the caravan; he was followed by Evelyn, while Lord Bannister brought up the rear following close the water-bearing camel which was hitched to his own mount by a short halter, for the path across the dangerous salt swamp was exactly two feet wide. Their progress was noisy for the path crunched beneath the camels' hooves and a cold, white mud would rise now and then from under its caked crust; this ancient slime is said to have been the bed of an ocean long ages ago.

It was a fine moonlit night. The *shott* gleamed faintly in the white light like the surface of a river covered with huge blocks of ice; it was even more bleak and desolate than the desert.

The camels would split and paw the ground, not wanting to go any farther. The cracked crust of salt hurt their hooves, and instinct told them that death was lying in wait for them here. Azrim had to use his stick frequently; the animals brayed and kicked.

Fear clutched Evelyn by the throat.

The wind stirred up the thin layer of salt that covered the swamp like powered dust, and swept it along in rustling clouds beside them.

Lord Bannister did not speak. He saw that the itinerary had been changed. But that was nothing unusual, of course. They had already abandoned the original plan. Now they were being followed again. There would be no stopping till they come to the Equator. And what sort of a state would they all be in then?

His face and hands were filmed over with a cold, sticky deposit of salt.

At one point the water-bearing camel stumbled from the path and began to struggle through the soft mud, braying hideously all the time. It was a miracle that Lord Bannister's own mount was not dragged after it by the halter tethering the two animals. Luckily, Lord Bannister had sufficient presence of mind to lean heavily backwards, pulling at the bridle with both hands until Azrim came to his assistance. The guide slashed the taut halter, then tried to pull the writhing animal out of the swamp.

It had already sunk into the mud as far as its belly, but their united strength was enough to drag it back somehow on to the firm path. In the meantime, Lord Bannister had stumbled and sunk up to his knees in the rotting weeds that bordered the track.

Evelyn looked imploringly towards Lord Bannister, in a silent appeal for forgiveness as he struggled back on to the path, his legs coated with the loathsome mud.

Lord Bannister sighed and made a deprecating gesture with one hand.

"It's a difficult thing to be a humanitarian, Miss Weston," he said. "Maybe I'll stop trying if I have to take many more of these journeys."

In the morning, worn out and covered with mud they arrived at Marbouk.

There were only two buildings in the oasis: A forbidding-looking adobe hut which served as an inn, and at a little distance, the painted block-house of the military convalescence camp. An Arab *douar* consisting of a few tents formed the main square of the place.

They asked for tea to be served immediately and while this was prepared they quickly changed into clean clothes. The need to have a shave never entered Lord Bannister's head, so keen was he on having a hot cup of tea.

As soon as breakfast was over, Evelyn rose from the table.

"I'm going straight to the hospital to hand the document over to the military authorities. I would like you to come with me."

Lord Bannister sighed.

"Forward, forward, all the time; it seems we must always be on the move. And once you've got going, there's no knowing when you can sit down again."

"I wish you'd stop brooding, Lord Bannister. Are you coming or are you not?"

"I am not. Now that you are here, you can't possibly go anywhere except to the only other building in the oasis, and that building is a military establishment. You couldn't possibly sally forth into the desert on foot, so I can safely let you go. Besides, I am beginning to believe you when you say that your mission *is* an honourable one. Don't know why. Perhaps this fellow Rancing had convinced me with his story about the house in the King's Road. I have confidence in you, Miss Weston. And so I am putting *my* honour, too, into your hand together with this envelope. Here you are."

He handed the case to her.

She looked at him earnestly.

"Thank you. You may rest assured that I'll guard your honour as jealously as I guard my own."

"Besides... I hope you don't mind... Er... I'd like to have a shave." He spoke anxiously, suspecting that she would resent his intention. God alone knew why she was so keen for him to grow a beard. And sure enough, her eyes flashed angrily.

"Ah! So that's what lies behind your newborn confidence in me! If your chin were smooth you would be certain to accompany me, wouldn't you? Under the circumstances, however, you are compelled to have confidence in me, since tidiness is, perhaps, even more important to you than honour."

Angrily, she walked out of the room and banged the door. Let the horrid man go and look for his razor! In the desert if he had mind to. She felt like crying. Most irritating of all was the knowledge that she did in fact love this horrible prig.

Lord Bannister went up to his room. Already the heat of the sun was scorching, and the walls of the adobe hut gave out a fusty smell. The matting was alive with vermin and everywhere there was the buzzing of insects. From downstairs came the incessant throaty chanting of the innkeeper, an Arab half-demented from too much hashish.

Poor girl. A trip like that behind her and she didn't even bother to take a rest. He felt ashamed of this own weariness and decided to do something to please her.

He would *not* shave!

Then she would realize, when she came back, that it was not because he had wanted to have a shave that he had let her go by herself. That was what he would do. Uncomfortable though it might be, to prove the genuineness of his trust in her, he would for the first time in his life disregard the stubble on his chin. Though from what he knew of her, he might well grow a beard that reached down to his waist before earning one word of approval from her.

He decided to go to bed. It seemed a very sensible procedure, for there was no knowing if he would be wakened or not, and perhaps even told to go on some long and urgent journey. The girl averred that their travels had come to an end, but a scientist must always weigh the evidence before agreeing to any statement and he had observed that on more than one occasion when he had felt free to enjoy a respite from worry, his freedom had turned out to be quite illusory.

Lord Bannister therefore decided to forego his shave and instead lay down on the mat to sleep.

·4·

There were eight patients in the neat and cheerful ward: eight convalescent soldiers with bronzed faces. They were chatting, playing cards and smoking. But one of their number was standing apart, his back turned to his comrades, looking out of the window.

There was a knock on the door and Evelyn entered the ward, saying clearly and firmly.

"I am looking for M. Münster."

The soldier who was standing by the window slowly turned round and looked at the visitor; there was an expression of lethargic indifference on his drawn and sickly face. The other convalescents turned in surprise and stared at the pretty girl with every indication of interest; Münster gave her the same blank stare which a moment before he had bestowed on the garden bench. It was not the unknowing regard of the mentally afflicted but the unfocused stare of someone whose thoughts were habitually turned towards the past and who now went through the motions of living like an automaton. His reply, drawling and soft, was nevertheless distinct:

"I am Münster. What can I do for you?"

"I am Lady...I mean I'm Miss...I wonder if you could come into the garden with me?"

"As you please."

He followed her with steady, measured strides.

She was overcome with nervousness and quite forgot her own troubles in her pity for Brandon. She was face to face with the principal character of a drama long since played out. His reason had not become clouded, but he was living the numbed existence of one who no longer feels anything. What should she tell him?

When they were alone together in the garden she began:

"I know who you are. Your real name is Brandon and you used to be a Lieutenant-Commander."

"Really." He spoke with polite indifference.

"I know your tragedy. Indeed, better than you do."

"Yes?" This too sounded hollow as when one strikes the same note on piano twice in succession.

"First of all, I have to inform you that your younger brother was innocent."

She was watching closely and saw him wince. So he could still feel and suffer. He frowned and looked at her severely.

"Who are you?"

"Someone who knows the truth about your case and who has come here to rehabilitate you. Your brother was just as innocent as you are. It was Wilmington, your brother-in-law, who did it."

Then she told him the whole story, from Miss Ardfern's betrayal of young Brandon to the farewell note which Wilmington had made use of after stealing the map. The soldier sat down and put a hand to his side as if his wound was troubling him.

"Yes", he said, musingly." Probably that is what happened. I don't know where you got the facts, but I believe you. However no one would believe *me*. But it's no longer of any importance to me, I assure you."

"If you were able to give back the stolen map intact, with the seals unbroken... Would that rehabilitate you?"

"That envelope has long since been passed on to certain people to whom it is extremely valuable and who have long since broken the seals and read the contents."

"Would you please answer my question? What would happen if you could bring a witness who would swear to the truth of what I have told you and produce the envelope with the seals unbroken?"

"Well, in that case... Well, then..." A gleam of interest appeared in his eyes, and his face kindled. "In that case not only could my innocence be proved, but I should render a service..."

"Here you are."

She handed him the envelope. As he started at it colour rose to his cheeks and brightness to his eyes. Then the brightness fell and splashed his tunic.

"Who are you?" he asked huskily; the envelope trembled in his hand.

"My name is Evelyn Weston. I am worth a hundred thousand francs—dead or alive."

She handed him the newspaper, which she had kept with the envelope in her small leather case.

After perusing the paper, Brandon sat in silent thought for some time.

"I wonder why you have gone to such trouble to bring me this means of proving my innocence. Why should you...?

"Because there is something *you* can do for *me*. I am looking for a small box surmounted by a ceramic statuette representing Buddha. You bought it from Messrs. Longson and North fifteen years ago."

"Buddha... Why, yes! I remember... I bought it for my elder brother as a Christmas gift. Of course! It's an enamelled box with a statuette of Buddha on the lid. He has a fancy for that kind of thing, you know."

"Who is your elder brother?"

"Lord Bannister... Why, what? I say, corporal! Bring some water! She's fainted! Quick!"

•5•

It was dusk when Evelyn and the soldier returned to the inn. The simple-minded, hashish-smoking innkeeper was squatting at the entrance, chanting the same three and a half notes as before. They learned from him that his lordship was not yet down.

They went upstairs, but at the door Evelyn stopped Brandon, saying, "Perhaps I had better prepare him for the news."

She knocked. There was no reply so she opened the door a little and peeped inside. His lordship, still wearing his clothes, was lying on the mat among the seething insects, and was fast asleep. He certainly looked both battered and exhausted.

She touched his shoulder, but he did not wake up.

Then she shook him vigorously and he opened his eyes. Immediately he recognized that he was in a similar situation and felt no surprise. Sadly, he heaved himself to his feet.

"We're leaving?" he asked, and started for the window. "Any ladder?"

"We aren't leaving for anywhere."

"Must we hide then?" he asked, a shade more sadly, but still without demur.

"Lord Bannister," she said with an unusual display of emotion which his lordship thought has been aroused by the sight of his stubby chin. "You will be pleased to see someone you haven't seen for a long time."

"I knew it! Holler has found his way here!"

"It's someone... a man... you lost touch with long ago." His face darkened a little, and he looked at her searchingly. "It is a man to whom you are very devoted. He is the same person for whose honour we have braved so many deadly perils."

She opened the door and Brandon entered the room.

It is only in old plays that on occasions like this people make elaborate tests to show that they are not dreaming. These two men did no such thing. Nor did they proclaim their relationship, firing at each other the one word "Brother!" for this was something that they had learnt in early youth. They embraced in silence, then clasped hands and spoke never a word.

It was some time before they felt calm enough to be able to say anything.

Evelyn, of course, had had no idea that the man with whom she had crossed the Channel was brother to the very Lieutenant-Commander Brandon she had set out to trace; and, thanks to Lord Bannister's aloofness and reserve, she had never had occasion to acquaint him with the facts.

"What do you propose to do now?" Lord Bannister asked his brother. "You must immediately set about clearing yourself of the charges of treason and dishonesty! Mustn't bear it a minute more."

"As a member of the Legion, I must report the case to Headquarters in Morocco. As the French are as interested in this map as the English, I hope they will not take the information through the usual official channels."

"Miss Weston..." Lord Bannister turned to Evelyn in embarrassment, and stroked his bristling chin. "I will now... I'll have to..."

She replied in a dignified and distant fashion.

"I hope you realize that it was really to restore someone's honour that I have troubled you now and then. I am sorry, after all, a gentleman's life is not a pub in which anyone can come in and go out as he pleases."

Brandon looked searchingly first at the girl then at his brother. He had never seen his brother looking as neglected and morose as this moment when he lowered his eyes, muttering some indistinguishable words.

"Oh, by the way," Brandon said abruptly. "Miss Weston is looking for some old family jewel..."

"I seem to have heard about that," Lord Bannister muttered, shuddering slightly.

"To find it, she will need that small box with a little statuette of a Buddha on it," Brandon continued. "I bought it for you as a Christmas present. You may remember..."

"Why didn't you say so?" exclaimed Lord Bannister enthusiastically. "The statuette and the box are at your disposal at any time, Miss Weston."

"The best idea would be for me to send a cable to my mother," she said excitedly, "and for you to instruct the staff at your place in London that they are to hand the Dreaming Buddha over to Mrs. Weston."

"It's absolutely unnecessary," Lord Bannister smiled. "We have the little Buddha with us here."

Evelyn's blood drummed wildly in her temples and chest.

"Where?"

"In my toilet case. He is sitting at this moment on top of my shaving kit... Why! Miss Weston! Quick, bring some water! She's fainted."

For the second time that day Evelyn fell to the floor unconscious.

•6•

The atmosphere was heavy with gloom. When the two men had listened to Evelyn's story of the perilous situation in which she had found herself, and of her wild flight, whose greatest thrills Lord Bannister had shared, the tragicomical aspect of the situation made them shudder.

She had thrown her fortune away with her own hand!

Her vendetta against Lord Bannister's toilet case had ended; and it was she who had been laid low.

"We'll send out search parties to comb the desert," Lord Bannister mumbled when he noticed the melancholy expression with which she was watching the antics of the centipedes on the floor of beaten clay.

Lord Bannister himself was aware that his suggestion was perfectly hopeless. It was ludicrous to think of trying to find a toilet case in the middle of the desert where the sand was driven by the wind into a new position every day, sometimes burying entire caravans in an hour.

Evelyn looked at the men with a strange, melancholy smile on her lips.

"No use crying over spilt milk," she said. "It was God' will that I went in search of the diamond and found the envelope. A soldier's honour is worth at least as much as the finest diamond."

"Your efforts, of course..."

"I hope, Lord Banister," she cut him off resolutely, "that you do not intend to offend me by offering me a 'fitting reward'?"

There was silence for some minutes before Lord Bannister burst out.

"The thing was within your reach all the time. Why, already on the channel boat, it was actually in the cabin with you. You would have left it in the road near Lyons, had I not insisted that we must drive back to get it! That's what women are. They will cheerfully throw something away a dozen times, but when it has really gone for good, then they realize that it was their most cherished treasure."

"That remark rivals your quotation from Aristotle," Evelyn remarked somewhat spitefully. She realized that there were times when he did not appreciate as he ought to have done, her attempt to restore his brother's honour. "I have an uncle who has a gift for coining better sayings than that. It's his opinion that many men are like a dress suit: absolutely useless when out of place."

Lord Bannister blushed.

"I, too, have incurred a grievous loss," he replied heatedly.

"I was fond of that shaving Buddha. And as for the dress suit, though a main road may not have been the proper place to wear it, I think I didn't give a bad account of myself."

"You wouldn't have come along with me, had it not been to save your skin."

"Miss Weston... you... you are being unfair!"

"Ungrateful was the word you wanted to say. Go ahead. Say it."

They chased each other round the room, hurling insults like two children. Lord Bannister even banged the table.

"Hurting each other won't do any good at all," Brandon opined.

They relapsed into silence. Evelyn wept. Lord Bannister muttered.

"It's time," Brandon said, "to settle this business of the envelope. I will now get through to Headquarters and make my report. We can't let you go on being wanted by police. My brother and I will testify that you have risked your life to recover this vital document for your country."

Suddenly, they heard the blast of a trumpet. The alarm was being sounded.

·7·

Before the days of wireless, lights were used to flash messages between the oases. On this particular evening lights were once again seen signaling in the distance:

It was an appeal for help, repeated some fifty times and those who sent the desperate message were clearly without a radio transmitter.

"Gangsters... raid... oasis... Marbouk... S.O.S... Gangsters... raid... oasis... Marbouk... S.O.S..."

The message was not only an appeal for help but also a warning of danger.

The garrison of five rounded up all the inhabitants into the fort-like military hospital: a few old Arabs, several children, some eight to ten invalid soldiers and the small garrison—not exactly a community which could be expected to put up a very strong resistance.

"Who can these raiders be?" wondered the Commanding Officer.

"Miss Weston and I can tell you that," Lord Bannister said calmly, accepting one of the rifles that were being distributed.

"It's a gang of common thieves and murderers plus a number of Arab marauders led by a spy who is wanted all over Europe and who goes by the name of Adams. We can expect that will number at least fifty men."

"In that case we're as good as dead."

"That's what I think, too," Lord Bannister agreed quietly.

·8·

Eddy Rancing was awakened by a nauseatingly evil smell. He felt a piece of hot wet meat moving over his face. He was being licked by a hyena.

He sat up in alarm. The hyena growled and jumped back. The young man summoned all his strength, whipped out his gun and drove the beast away by firing a number of shots.

The heat was intense, the sun blazing mercilessly over the parched desert. His head was aching and there was a huge swelling on the place where he had been hit. He struggled to his feet, and started to stagger forward scarcely conscious of what he was doing.

Behind an unusually high sand-dune he found enough shadow to be able to sit out of the sun's rays. He bowed his aching head and copped his chin in his palms.

It was the end.

It was going to be a rather hackneyed death. Desert, thirst and all that. He might have guessed. Everything had gone wrong from the very start. This was what came of running after diamonds…

He was breathing with difficulty, for the dust irritated his lungs; his tongue became swollen and his lips, also swollen, became chapped. His skin began to itch unbearably as all the moisture evaporated almost visibly from his body. "Water makes up two-thirds of the human body," he remembered from his lessons at school. These two-thirds would evaporate here pretty soon. Then he would be lying in the sand, a shrivelled corpse, like those of the medieval monks that were hung in their cassocks on the walls of the vaults of ancient monasteries.

He began to gasp for water; half-mad with thirst, he started off once more into the desert. The enormous disc of the sun was veiled now behind clouds of yellow dust and was beginning to sink towards the horizon where there was an area of peculiar radiance in which human figures mounted on camels were moving upside down.

Eddy, stumbling and faltering, walked on until the sun exploded in a blaze of violet and disappeared behind the farthest sand-dunes.

He stumbled and fell full length to the ground. He had not the strength to rise again. He crept on his stomach towards the dark object which had tripped him up and picked up a leather toilet case.

With trembling hands he snapped it open, thinking only that it might contain water. As he fumbled with the case the moon appeared and shed a faint glow across the sky. Then Eddy lifted out of the case a large smooth object which he set down in the dust so that he could examine it.

Eddy Rancing found himself eyeing the Dreaming Buddha! There he was, sitting on top of his enamelled box; his head bowed as if he was ashamed of the whole business. They had met at journey's end: in the Sahara.

You got what you deserved, Eddy Rancing, he thought. Not for nothing have you endured all these hardships. There! It's yours now! Drink it!

For he knew that this was the real thing. This one contained the diamond and no mistake. Why he felt so sure was not important; but he had no doubt whatever! He had only to give it a sharp knock against some rock, and the diamond would be revealed.

Eddy Rancing began to shriek with laughter. He rolled on his back in the dust of the desert, flung his arms wide, and laughed at the top of his voice; he laughed hideously, his face distorted by a thousand wrinkles.

The Buddha watched him silently.

•9•

After midnight, when the sand of the Sahara, having made haste to give out the heat it had absorbed during the day, becomes almost as cold as ice, Eddy Rancing revived. Death does not come so easily in the desert; when the atmosphere is cooler, there is less evaporation of humidity from the body and remaining fluids start circulating once again. Thus nature forced Eddy into a renewed consciousness of his terrible position.

He could see the Buddha sitting motionless in front of him, head bowed as if watching over his death. But he felt indifferent to his fate. He reached his hand into the toilet case and pulled out a convex mirror, a comb, a torch, a book, a shaving stick...and a bottle!

Quickly he unscrewed the cap of the bottle and sniffed the mildly mentholated fragrance of its contents. He drained the bottle in one gulp. He had never had a more delicious drink than this half pint of lukewarm Harris & Crompton gargle. Little did Messrs. Harris & Crompton dream that Edward Rancing would one day rate their "mildly aromatic Dandy gargle" higher than every kind of cocktail, wine and champagne.

He revived sufficiently to be able to sit up. He seemed to feel the gargle coursing through his veins. And its mildly mentholated aroma was indeed refreshing.

He took hold of the Buddha, intending to smash the little statuette. However, he changed his mind. That diamond might as well stay where it was until he was once again in a safe place. The thought of the diamond reminded him of Oasis Marbouk, Evelyn and the gangsters. He remembered that the gangsters were about to raid the oasis where Evelyn and Lord Bannister would now be resting, all unaware that death was marching towards them.

He wondered idly what he could do to help them and immediately the answer flashed into his mind. It had not been for nothing that he had flirted with a lighthouse-keeper's daughter. He looked wryly at the Buddha and thought that here in the Sahara you had to be ready to acquire a new set of valves. It was the Morse Code, not the diamond, that would be most useful to him now.

He switched on the torch, and held the mirror in front of it. Then, just as he had learned from grim Pop Harrington's daughter, he alternately covered the magnifying mirror and held it against the light, thus producing the letters of the Morse alphabet: short, long, short; short, long, short...

The signals could be seen miles away in the darkness.

"Gangsters... raid... oasis... Marbouk... S.O.S..."

He kept on signalling until the mirror dropped from his hand and he rolled over, exhausted. With the last ounce of his strength he turned the torch so that its beam was directed perpendicularly into the sky. That was what saved his life.

"That's where the signals came from! Look at that long shaft of light!" exclaimed P. J. Holler, who now had a leather bag slung round his neck, since camels, like aeroplanes, had a rather depressing effect on him.

•10•

Outside the fortress-hospital, the gangsters were somewhat checked by the first volley from within. About half a dozen Arabs dismounted head first from their camels.

"Get back!" Adams yelled.

The raiders fell back among the palm-trees and opened fire from this cover.

A bullet hit the window-frame beside Lord Bannister's head, and sent splinters of wood flying in every direction. Lord Bannister did not bat an eyelid but went on firing. Only when Evelyn screamed softy, he glanced in her direction.

"Now you can see, Miss Weston, that a gentleman can wield other weapons besides his razor. I recall how during the war—they can certainly shoot," he muttered, somewhat surprised. He did not finish telling her what had happened in the war.

The gangsters were firing sporadically. There was no doubt but that they were working to a plan, and this was soon revealed. The ward filled with a peculiar, acrid smell.

"Something's burning!" cried the Commanding Officer.

An Arab came running in.

"Some cursed dog has got behind the building and thrown a lighted torch unto the roof!"

They could hear a crackling noise like the rattle of a machine-gun. The fire was spreading, and there was no possibility of them being able to put it out since anyone who ventured to expose himself on the roof would be a sitting target for the enemy.

"Miss Weston," Lord Bannister said, "you may need this."

He handed her an automatic.

"Thank you, "she said.

Flames were shooting from the roof; the room filled with smoke which became so dense that they could scarcely breathe. Rats scurried between the feet of the defenders.

"The envelope!" cried Brandon; the others were coughing so much that they could not speak.

Lord Bannister understood what was in his brother's mind. The envelope would have to be destroyed to prevent it from falling into the gangsters' hands.

Bullets rained into the room as the gangsters prepared for a general assault. There was the crash of shattered glass as the window-panes fell in and the thud of overturned furniture. Lord Bannister, holding his lighter, edged his way towards the envelope with the five seals, which Brandon was holding up so that his brother could put a light to it.

Evelyn, deathly pale, was standing with her back to the wall, clutching her Browing. A bullet pierced the medicine-chest next to her head but she did not even notice. Her gaze was riveted on the envelope, and her heart was heavy. The envelope would be destroyed and they would all die. The whole undertaking had been in vain.

But in the second before Lord Bannister could flick on his lighter, all were startled by a sudden volley of firing close at hand and the simultaneous peal of a bugle.

A troop of fierce spahis had arrived on the scene, led by a tame editor wearing a leather bag suspended round his neck.

·11·

When a photograph of Miss Evelyn Weston appeared in all the morning papers, P. J. Holler almost choked. He was eating fried fish when he noticed it and a mouthful went down the wrong way.

He recognized the face as that of Lady Bannister. He was at first dumbfounded to think that Lady Bannister could be an intelligence agent. And it was inconceivable to think of her as a burglar and a murderer. And yet, and yet... he remembered that it had been on the very evening of the envelope robbery that she had turned up with her dress torn and spattered with mud. He remembered that Lord Bannister had nearly choked when he had been shown the newspaper account in the plane from Lyons. And why had that pedantic peer dressed up as a Tyrolese folk singer? And there were other unanswered questions too.

What could he possibly do? He was absolutely certain that Evelyn Weston and Lady Bannister were one and the same person. But he could not afford to discount the remote chance that this was not so.

"Careful, Peter Jerry," he told himself. "Keep your wits about you."

He would have to go after her. Where was it that she had gone to? Oh, yes. Oasis Marbouk! But first he would have to go and see Lord Bannister.

At Lord Bannister's villa, he was told that the scientist had left in the company of a lady and a visitor. The valet, new in Lord Bannister's employ, could not tell him whether or not the lady was his lordship's wife.

"Look here, my man, "P. J. Holler said nervously. "You're not a stranger in this town. I want you to go out and hire twenty reliable men who would be willing to come with me immediately to Oasis Marbouk. I want to go to your master's assistance, as I believe he is in danger. Here are five hundred francs in advance."

Within an hour, the valet had the caravan ready, complete with guide, water-carrier and provisions; and he had attached himself to the rescue party too.

Thus P. J. Holler set out to do his own detective work. The questions to which he wanted an answer were:

a) Who is Münster, the man Evelyn Weston has been looking for?

b) Are Lady Bannister and Evelyn Weston one and the same person?

If so, what is Lord Bannister's connection with the affair? If she *was* a spy, then he, P. J. Holler, intended to run her to earth as well as all her cronies. What a headline! If she was not a spy, he would claim to be visiting Oasis Marbouk, which he had every right to do, and he would in no way lose face. He scarcely contemplated the idea of informing the police. He felt that his position as a British newspaper man entitled him to the right to make his own investigations. If he failed, then the detectives could take on the job.

And as there is a special guardian angel to protect journalists on their journeys, P. J. Holler ran into a detachment of spahis by the ruins of the ancient Latin city in the desert. Nor was this enough. The officer in charge of the spahis turned out to be Lieutenant Villers, an old acquaintance of his from the time of the Riff War, when he had worked at General Headquarters as a war correspondent!

"Hello, Holler!" the lieutenant greeted him. "Why, you look like a real Bedouin out of the latest revue of the Follies Bergères."

"Hello, Villers! What on earth are you doing in a Latin city where the night-clubs have been closed for the last thousand years and there's no jazz?"

"Patrol, sir. Forty-eight hours on patrol duty. Where are you heading for?"

"I'm going to Oasis Marbouk. I'm on holiday, and I'm going everywhere where I've no business to be."

"Then allow me to provide a gala escort for the British press. I'll see you as far as the desert well."

But when darkness fell Lieutenant Villers did not return to his base. From that moment, the detachment of spahis rode hell for leather onwards, together with P. J. Holler, for the officer had seen and interpreted the light signals.

On the way, they found Eddy Rancing, whom Lord Bannister's valet and a few of the Arabs escorted back to the town. The spahis, led by a harassed P. J. Holler, pushed on towards Marbouk at breakneck speed.

They were just in time.

Gordon, Dr. Cournier and Beefy were killed by the first volley. The others, including Adams, were handcuffed. Rainer was still giving off an offensive smell, which made it impossible for him to be questioned at the moment. As they tied him up by the wrists, he said resignedly:

"I have never before had a wish come true so quickly. All day long, I have been wishing I could stay in some cool place for a good long time. It certainly looks as though my wish will come true this time."

And it did.

·12·

For the first time in his life, Lord Bannister truly meant the phrase he had so often repeated on previous occasions merely out of politeness:

"I'm very glad to see you, my dear Holler."

The editor rolled his eyes and breathed heavily.

"Gimme some pickles… or a lemon. Damn that camel. He was rocking so vehemently there were times I thought I'd go down between his humps. Gimme some pickles."

In the meantime, Lieutenant Villers had got through to G.H.Q. and G.H.Q. called the British Embassy in Paris, and both Legionary Münster-Brandon and Lord Bannister spoke on the line, too.

Then the caravan set out on the return journey to Marrakesh. It was headed by Lord Bannister and his brother, Evelyn with her leather-bag, and P. J. Holler (who had obtained an abundant supply of pickled gherkins). Holler knew that with his usual luck he had landed one of his big scoops. Lord Bannister had promised to tell him all that he thought could be safely divulged to the public, and had given his hand on it that Holler had an option on the story.

Once again they were assembled in the drawing-room of Lord Bannister's villa. All round the house and garden spahis were strolling as if by chance. The gangsters were now being questioned. Telephone messages were received and transmitted, and Evelyn was interviewed by military intelligence officers. Once her part in the affair had been elucidated, her exploits were invested with glory. However, Evelyn was sitting tired and dispirited in Lord Bannister's drawing-room in which a fireplace added national atmosphere to a room which was already furnished in a uniquely British style; it was a strange room to find in Africa.

Evelyn was saddened by the thought of all the hardships she had endured in vain.

"A rotten business," Lord Bannister remarked sadly.

"What business?" Holler inquired, sniffing like the newshound that he was.

"Oh, nothing," said Lord Bannister. "I've lost my shaving kit. A small enamelled box. Very distressing. Used to be there on the mantelpiece, and..."

He flung an arm casually in the direction of the mantelpiece, turned his head, and remained in this position as if frozen. His jaw dropped and everyone looked in the direction to which he was pointing.

Sitting with bowed head on the lid of an enamelled box on the mantelpiece, was the Dreaming Buddha.

Lord Bannister, Evelyn and Brandon rose as one man and started towards the object as if mesmerised. Lord Bannister was the first to lay his hand on it. Then they all stood as if transfixed.

"Why, that's your shaving kit all right, Lord Bannister," exclaimed P. J. Holler. "We found it lying beside the open toilet case where we picked up that young man. It looked as if he had known what to do with your gargle. Your toilet case saved his life, and he saved our lives with his torch. Your valet brought the young man here and, of course, he brought home everything that young gentleman had failed to make use of. I won't go bail for anything except the shaving block, though."

But no one was listening to P. J. Holler. Three pairs of gleaming eyes stared at the Buddha. That was what had saved them all!

But what could an oriental prophet expect in return for a miracle he had wrought? Not gratitude. As the parable tells us, he could not even expect that in his own country. They noted the fact that he had saved their lives by way of a miracle. Then—then they dashed it with all their might to the floor so that it broke into a thousand pieces.

Just as the aged convict had imagined in his dreams, the diamond sparkled out of the ruined statuette. They rubbed the clay from it and the diamond was revealed in all its fabulous beauty. Four pairs of eyes looked at it as if mesmerised, much as the late Jim Hogan had looked at it when Prince Radovsky handed it to him with a princely gesture.

•13•

During the next twelve hours there were many urgent telephone calls to be made between Marrakesh, Paris and London. The military alliance between France and Britain rendered the matter as vital to the French authorities as it was to the British. As a result of these telephone calls, a certain member of the Legion by the name of Münster was declared by the medical officer to be unfit for military service because of his wound, and the legionary was demobilized forthwith. The very same day he flew to London, taking with him, in his attaché case, an orange-coloured envelope sealed with five seals.

Miss Evelyn Weston was front-page news in the French newspapers. She was their heroine. Miss Weston had risked her life to save a military document of such importance that if it had been lost it could not have been replaced. Pursued by the French police, she had evaded them that she might hand the document intact to the military authorities who could best deal with it. Miss Weston and Wilmington (who had since been killed) had provided evidence which had established the innocence of the unfortunate Lieutenant-Commander Brandon and cleared him of the charge of espionage.

It was Brandon who had been used by that same Wilmington who had been murdered in his Paris flat. All this had been endorsed by evidence taken from the dangerous spy Adams, who had been arrested in the Sahara.

Miss Weston had produced witnesses and documentary evidence to prove that she had called at the deceased Wilmington's place in quest of her rightful legacy. A British Naval court-martial was meeting to examine the case of Lieutenant-Commander Brandon, who had voluntarily asked to have his case re-opened. It was confidently expected that as a result of the enquiry Brandon would be rehabilitated.

·14·

Evelyn and Lord Bannister were hovering, somewhat irresolutely, in a shady corner of the garden. For some time now they had been lingering there chatting idly and absent-mindedly.

Each was thinking of the other.

At last, Lord Bannister cleared his throat and spoke.

"Do you think you can forgive me?"

"I cannot."

She is paying me back in my own coin, he thought, and was at a loss what to say next.

"Can you remember by any chance," he went on at last, "the name of the village where I wanted to sleep that night? I would like to return the innkeeper's dressing-gown. He may be in need of it, poor fellow."

"You can give it to me. I can call in there on my way home. It's called La Roselle. I'm sure I'm not likely to forget the name."

"I say, why can't you forgive me? Such cold-heartedness is not becoming in a young lady, you know."

"I cannot possibly forgive you because you haven't offended me, Henry. Have I your permission to address you like that in Holler' absence?"

"I would much rather have you use my title...Ahem... What do you think? I think it's a bit cold out here. I mean to say..." His lordship was overcome with embarrassment.

However, his embarrassment diminished when Evelyn placed both her hands on his shoulders. Then they looked wonderingly into each other's eyes.

•15•

Eddy Rancing came off best among the participants of this adventure. Having sown his wild oats, he sobered down. First he was feted as the hero of Oasis Marbouk. Messrs. Harris & Crompton paid him five thousand pounds for an advertisement in which he told the world that he owed his life solely to the mildly aromatic Dandy gargle. ("Indispensable in deserts.") In another statement, Mr. Rancing eulogised the "high nutritive value of the Dandy Vitamin Cream".

He agreed to stay in Africa as Lord Bannister's private secretary, the most prudent decision of his life.

In the highways and byways of London, eyebrows were often raised at the approach of an impeccably dressed white-haired gentleman carrying a horsewhip and obviously searching for someone. This gentleman was looking for Edward Frederic George Henry Rancing, and his own name was Mr. Arthur (Bede Cecil David) Rancing. He had fled from Mügli am See, Switzerland one stormy night leaving his luggage behind; and Mrs. Grete Rancing (née Wollishoff) was sitting, surrounded by her cats, hourly expecting his return.

•16•

All were assembled at Lord Bannister's house in London. His lordship had returned with his young wife from their honeymoon barely twenty-four hours earlier. Among those present were the rehabilitated Lieutenant-

Commander Brandon and Mrs. Weston. In the evening of her life, she had found perfect happiness. Also present was Mr. Marius Bradford, authoritative and sound of judgement as ever.

Everyone was agreed that Lady Evelyn was the loveliest wife in the world. Lord Bannister thought her even lovelier than that.

Again and again, they recounted every detail of the extraordinary adventure. They were at once cheerful and sad, but, as a matter of fact, very happy.

"Isn't it all strange?" said Mrs. Weston. "What a lot of links had to be forged before we could complete the chain of circumstances that has finally brought us here."

"And to what end?" the Lieutenant-Commander asked, meditatively. "Where is the philosopher who can answer that?"

"I am a medical man," Lord Bannister said, looking at Lady Evelyn. "But we have in our family an outstanding intellect and I'm sure you can have an answer to your question."

But Mr. Bradford took this as a reference to himself and answered slowly, weighing his words,

"Life is like the waistcoat of a summer suit—short and pointless."